I0619071

THE TOMB OF TS'IN

THE TOMB OF TS'IN

EDGAR WALLACE

The Just Crimes of Tillizinni

Originally published in 1918.
Published by Wildside Press, LLC.
Visit us online at wildsidepress.com.

INTRODUCTION

KARL WURF

Edgar Wallace (1875–1932) was one of the most widely read popular writers of his era, producing more than 170 novels and hundreds of short stories, plays, and screenplays. Born in London to working-class parents, he worked as a soldier and journalist before becoming a novelist. Wallace absorbed the energy of late Victorian penny dreadfuls and serialized adventure tales, carrying their pace and melodrama into his own work. He was influenced by Arthur Conan Doyle's detective stories, Sax Rohmer's "Yellow Peril" thrillers, and the wider tradition of imperial adventure writing that cast far-off lands as stages for mystery and intrigue.

During the 1910s and 1920s, Wallace was one of the most popular writers in Britain, so much so that publishers claimed one in four books sold bore his name. His work helped define the modern thriller, blending crime, exotic settings, and secret societies with an eye for cliffhanger suspense. The Tomb of Ts'in (1918) belongs to this vein of exotic adventure, drawing on Western fascination with China and the legend of the First Emperor's buried treasure. It mixes international conspiracy, daring adventurers, and hidden knowledge in a way that typifies Wallace's appeal at the height of his career.

Wallace's popularity, however, did not last. After his death in 1932, crime and mystery fiction shifted toward psychological depth and logical puzzles, led by writers like Agatha Christie and Dorothy L. Sayers. Wallace's melodramatic villains, breathless pacing, and imperial attitudes quickly came to seem old-fashioned. Today, he is remembered less for his literary refinement than for his sheer productivity and influence on popular storytelling. The Tomb of Ts'in offers a vivid glimpse of the style that once gripped millions of readers, and of an author whose energy helped pave the way for the modern thriller.

INTRODUCTORY

HAD Tillizinni written this story of the tomb of Ts'in Hwang Ti (the King of Ts'in who became Emperor literally) from the notes he had upon the case, it might have made a greater and a better book.

You would have pardoned such extravagance of style as he displayed in his extraordinary narrative, remembering that he is of Italian birth and that English is too full of pitfalls to the foreigner for his liking. For of truth, though Tillizinni speaks and writes the three Arabics, Moorish (which I think is the purest), Turkish, and Russian, with considerable fluency, and though he knows at least seven dialects in the Chinese tongue, and can converse in most of the modern languages, yet English, with its bland and inviting simplicity, is a tongue which more than any other baffles and overawes him.

They say of Nicholo Tillizinni, his predecessor in the chair of Anthropology at Florence, and the benefactor and more than father, whose name Tillizinni bears, that he spoke all languages save Welsh; but I have reason for believing that he never completely mastered the niceties of our tongue.

Particularly did Tillizinni wish to write clearly in this story which I now tell (by his favour and at his request), for it is a story like none other I have ever heard or read.

It concerns the tomb of the Great Emperor—the first Emperor of the Chinese, who died two centuries before the birth of Christ; it concerns that extraordinary genius and adventurer, Captain Ted Talham—surely the most talkative man in the world; it concerns, too, that remarkable woman, Yvonne Yale, and last but not least, The Society of Joyful Intention—the most bloodthirsty organisation the world has known. It concerns Tillizinni also, for Scotland Yard placed him on his mettle, set him a challenging task, which threatened at one time to bring ruin to the greatest detective in Europe.

That it likewise brought him within an ace of losing his life, I should not think it worth while mentioning at this stage, but for the fact that scoffers might suppose that he held life dearer than fame.

Tillizinni has never greatly interested himself in Chinese affairs, and though he had been instrumental in bringing many men to their doom, yet, curiously enough, none of these have been inmates of the Celestial Kingdom; so that he welcomed with the welcome which a blasé mind offers to anything in the shape of novelty, the invitation of Scotland Yard to make himself acquainted with the Society of Joyful Intention. The story proper which is set forth here, begins with the surrounding of the China Packet.

On the 24th of November, in the year of the great storm, there went aground off the Goodwin Sands the China-Orient liner *Wu-song*. She was a modern steamer of six thousand tons, built by the Fanfield Company in 1900, and she traded between London and the China Sea. On the night in question she was homeward bound and was coming up the Channel at half speed, a precaution taken by her skipper as a result of a slight and patchy fog which lay on the Channel.

Off St. Margarets, for some unaccountable reason, she shifted her course, and before anybody seemed to realise what was happening, she was aground. No sea was running at the time, the storm, it will be remembered, occurred a fortnight later, and with the aid of two Dover tugs she was refloated.

That would seem rather a matter for the Trinity Masters than for Scotland Yard, but for the fact that in the natural excitement attendant upon the grounding, a very determined attempt was made to force the Stubb safe in the captain's cabin. Here again Scotland Yard might have dismissed the matter as a mere commonplace attempt to secure the safe's contents by some person or persons unknown, but for the fact that this was the third attempt which had been made during the voyage.

Coming through the Suez Canal the captain had been on the bridge—as is usual when a ship is making progress through the great waterway. He had left his steward in charge of his cabin, with instructions not to leave the apartment until he (the captain) returned. Half way through the Canal, with the ship's searchlights showing, and a clear stretch of water before him, he had snatched a moment to go to his cabin to get a muffler, for the night was cold.

The cabin was on the boat deck and inaccessible to passengers except by invitation. To his surprise he had found the big room in darkness and had put one foot over the weather board to enter the cabin, when two men rushed past him, knocking him over in their hurry. He called for a quarter-master, entered the cabin, and discovered his steward lying gagged and bound on the floor.

The man had been sitting reading when he had found himself violently seized and gagged by two men, one of whom had switched out the light the moment the assault was made.

The steward struggled, but he was powerless in the hands of his assailants, and for a quarter of an hour he lay upon the floor, his back to the intruders, whilst they attacked the safe.

One cannot say, without reflecting upon an eminent firm of safe-makers, whether the burglary would have succeeded but for the captain's return, but certain it is that the strangers had gone to work in a most scientific manner, and had made amazing progress in the short space of time.

The second attempt was made when the ship was two days out of Gibraltar, and was a half-hearted effort to blow open the door of the safe whilst the captain was conducting Church Service in the saloon. No guard had been left in the cabin, the captain thinking that the thieves would be scared at making any further attack, and, too, that they would hardly venture in broad daylight. Again they were disturbed and decamped unseen, leaving two pencils of nitro-glycerine to indicate their intentions.

Nor was the third, and final, and—one may suppose—desperate attempt any more successful; but this time the thieves were nearly caught. Captain Talham had seized his revolver the moment the ship went aground, for his crew was in the main Chinese, and he took no risks of a panic. When going back to his cabin to secure a lifebelt, he met the two indefatigable thieves, and there was a sharp exchange of shots.

This time the thieves were armed also. Again they evaded him and escaped in the fog.

Scotland Yard sent Tillizinni to interview the captain at the London docks, and he found him an average type of British seaman, kindly and communicative.

"The rum thing is," he explained, "that there was no money in the safe—not so much as a brass farthing."

"What did the safe contain?" asked Tillizinni.

He took up a sheet of paper from his desk and read:

"Ship's papers in envelope—confidential report on the working of the new condenser—and a green mailbag," he said.

Tillizinni was interested.

"Green mailbag?"

The captain nodded.

"That's the Ambassador's bag and is brought from the Court of Pekin to the ship by special messenger, and taken from me in London by a man from the Embassy."

"You see," he explained, "the Chinese Government always sends its mails like that—its Embassy mails, I mean. I bring 'em every trip. They don't trust the Embassy despatches over the Trans-Siberian Railway. They think that the Russians go through 'em."

"I see," said Tillizinni.

It was very clear what the objective had been. The green mailbag offered an irresistible temptation to somebody who knew its contents.

"There was nothing else?"

He shook his head.

"Nothing," he said.

There was little to do save to continue inquiries at the Chinese Embassy. Here, however, Tillizinni met with a check. A letter from the Embassy informed him that nothing of the slightest importance was contained in the bag. The letter continued:

"In this particular mail there were no official documents whatever, the bag being made up of a number of his Excellency's personal effects. These were in the nature of rare Chinese documents which his Excellency had sent for from his home in Che-foo, to assist him in the writing of an article which he is preparing for the *North American Review*. As Signor Tillizinni may know, his Excellency is an enthusiastic student of Chinese history, and has the finest private collection of historical documents relating to China in the world."

This letter came to Tillizinni at a moment when he had ample time to devote to the elucidation of the problem.

Our Italian friend was and is a peculiar man. He credited thieves of persistent characters, such as these men undoubtedly possessed, with intelligence out of the ordinary.

Whosoever made the attempt upon the safe of the China boat were well aware of the "worthlessness" of the safe's contents, and it was apparent that, worthless or not, the burglars had decided that to have them was worth the risk.

The passenger list was a small one, but it took a week to sort them out and establish their innocence. For the most part they were Customs officials and British officers returning home on leave; and the week-end found me with only two "doubtfuls."

The first of these was almost beyond suspicion. A Mr. de Costa, a ship-owner of sorts, was one, and Captain Talham was another.

Mr. de Costa, whom Tillizinni visited was, I should imagine, descended from a Portuguese family. A short, stout man, rather yellow of face, and bearing traces of his descent. He seemed the last person in the world to be suspected of commonplace felony.

Of Captain Talham, only fragmentary information was obtainable. He had apparently held a commission in a regiment of Irregular Horse during the South African war, and at the conclusion of hostilities he had gone to China in search of the adventure which at that time the great empire offered.

Beyond the fact that he had gone to China as far inland as Lau-tcheu; that he had been arrested later at Saigon in Cochin China, over some dispute with a French naval officer, and that he had a few months in Kuala Kangsan in Perak, little could be learnt about him. Later Tillizinni was destined to meet him, and discover much at first hand, for just as there was none so perfectly acquainted with his life, so there was none as willing to talk so freely about Captain Talham—as Captain Talham.

Here, then, with the conclusion of Tillizinni's unsatisfactory inquiries, the incident of the China Packet might have closed and have been relegated to the obscurity which is reserved for petty felonies, but for the events which followed the publication of the Ambassador's article.

From hereon I tell the story, suppressing nothing save that which may appear too flattering to Tillizinni. Such of the events which Tillizinni did not actually witness, I have written from information afforded me by the principal actors in this strangest of modern dramas.

* * * *

Here let me say one word about the title which heads this chapter. I have lumped together many acts of Signor Tillizinni and have described them as "Just Crimes," and I think that I have excellent reason for so describing them.

Tillizinni has always been a law unto himself. He worked on the solid basis that society was a lamb which must at all costs be protected from the wolves of the world, and to afford that protection he invoked the law of that land in which he was residing.

Sometimes the written law did not exactly cover a case, or presented a loop-hole through which an evil-doer might crawl unscratched. Tillizinni filled the hole—unlawfully. It was always better for a criminal to take his chance with the law than to take a chance with Tillizinni—that I know; that also many villains discovered too late for the knowledge to be of practical service.

CHAPTER 1

CAPTAIN TED TALHAM.

A MAN walked carelessly through Hyde Park with the air of one who had no destination. He was tall and straight, his shoulders were thrown back, his chin had that upward lift which seems part of the physiognomy of all who have followed a soldier's career. His face, lean and well-featured, was tanned with the tan of strong suns and keen cold winds, and though the day was chilly and a boisterous breeze swept across the bare spaces of the Park, he wore neither overcoat nor muffler. The upturned moustache and the shaggy eyebrows suggested truculence; the threadbare suit, for all its evidence of pressing and ironing, suggested that he had found patches of life none too productive.

A close examination might have revealed little darns at the extremities of his trousers, for he had a trick of brushing his heels together as he walked—a trick disastrous to garments already enduring more than their normal share of wear.

He walked carelessly, swinging his gold-headed malacca cane—incongruously magnificent—and whistling softly and musically as he moved.

The Park was almost deserted, for it was dusk, and the weather conditions were neither ideal nor inviting. Occasionally the gusty wind bore down a flake or two of snow and the skies overhead were sullen and grey.

He had reached the Ranger's House before he examined a cheap metal watch, which was affixed to his person by no more pretentious guard than a broad ribbon, bearing a suspicious resemblance to a lady's shoe-lace.

The watch had stopped—he arrested his progress to wind it, deliberately and with great earnestness. This done, he continued his stroll, bearing down towards the Serpentine.

He stood for a few moments cheerfully contemplating the dreary stretch of water, and three sad water-fowl, which came paddling toward him in the hope of sustenance, paddled away again, sadder than ever, for he offered no greater assistance to life than a cheerful chirrup.

He turned as a sharp footstep came to him from the gravelled path. A girl was walking quickly toward him from the Kensington end of the Park. Something in her face attracted his attention—if ever fear was written in a human countenance it was written in hers. Then, into view round a clump of bushes, came three men. They were small of stature, and it needed no second glance to tell him their nationality, for despite their European dress and their hard Derby hats, they wore their clothes in the négligé style which the Oriental alone can assume.

The girl saw the tall man and came towards him.

"I'm so sorry to trouble," she said breathlessly, "but these men have been following me for two days—but never so openly——"

She stopped and appeared to be on the verge of tears.

He bowed, a little slyly, and glanced at the three Chinamen, who now stood a dozen paces away, as though uncertain as to what was the next best move.

With a jerk of his head he beckoned them, and after a moment's consultation they obeyed the gesture.

"What do you want?" he asked.

"No savee," lisped one of the men. "No savee them pidjin."

He exchanged a few rapid sentences with his companions and a smile flickered momentarily at the corner of the tall man's mouth and vanished.

"What for you walkee this piecee lady all same time?" he asked.

Again the sotto-voce conference and the leader of the three shook his head.

"No makee walkee samee time," he said. "Makee walkee John allee samee, piecee lady no b'long."

The tall man nodded. He took from his waistcoat pocket a light blue porcelain disc and laid it on the palm of his hand and the three Chinamen walked nearer and examined it. They were puzzled by the demonstration.

"No savee," said the spokesman.

Captain Talham replaced the button in his pocket.

"Why do you follow this lady, you dogs?" he asked quickly, and the men shrank back, for he spoke in the hissing Cantonese dialect.

"Excellent lord," said the speaker humbly, "we are magnificent students walking as is our custom in the evening, and we have not the felicity of having seen this gracious and beautiful lady before."

"You lie," said the tall man calmly; "for if that were so, why did you say, 'Let us go away until this pig is out of sight, and then we will follow the woman?'"

The man he addressed was silent.

"Now you shall tell me what you mean," said Captain Talham and drew from his pocket the sky-blue button, fingering it thoughtfully.

This time the men saw and understood, and, as if at a signal, they bowed low, recognising in the inquisitor a mandarin of the Fourth or Military Class.

"Great mandarin," said one of the three who had not spoken. "We are servants of others, and it is said that 'the wise servant is dumb when the bamboo falls and dumb till he dies, when he is dumb for ever.'"

The tall man nodded.

"You shall give me your *hong* that I may know you," he said.

After a little hesitation, the man who was evidently the leader, took a little ivory cylinder from his pocket, and unscrewed it so that it came into two equal portions. The cylinder was no larger than a thick pencil and less than two inches long. One half was made up of an inking pad and at the end of the other was a tiny circular stamp.

Captain Talham held out the palm of his hand and the other impressed upon it the tiny Chinese character which stood for his name. One by one his fellows followed suit, though they knew that death might be the result of their disclosure.

The tall man examined the name carefully.

"'Noble Child,'" he read, "'Hope of the Spring,' and 'Star above the Yamen.'"

He nodded his head.

"You may go," said he; and with two little jerky bows the men turned and walked quickly in the direction from whence they had come.

He had time now to observe the girl, a grave and bewildered spectator of the scene. She was a little above medium height, and slight. Her hair was bronze-red and her face singularly beautiful. The skin was clear and white— so white as almost to suggest fragility. Her eyes were big and grey, and the two curved eyebrows, so sharp of line as to recall the pencilled brows which the mid-Victorian poet popularised, were dark, and contrasted with the glowing glory of the hair above. The nose was inclined to be retroussé, and the lips were faultless in shape and a warm red.

She presented the effect which the beautifiers of the world strive to attain, yet fail, for here nature had, in some mysterious fashion, blended all colourings in a harmony. She was well dressed, expensively so. Her simple gown suggested the studied simplicity which has made one Paris house famous the world over; and there was luxury in the furs about her throat and in the huge muff which was suspended with one hand.

"I don't know how to thank you," she began; and indeed she was in some embarrassment, for whilst he was obviously a gentleman, he was as obviously a very poor gentleman.

He smiled and there was good comradeship and the ease which begets friendship in the brief glimpse of even white teeth.

"In this world," he said, with no apparent effort at oratory, "existence is made tolerable by opportunity, and no aspect of opportunity is so coveted as that which afforded a gentleman to secure the safety, the peace of mind, or the happiness of a lady."

It was oratorical all right: there could be no doubt as to that, but there was no effort, no shaming after effect, no labour of delivery. He was neither self-conscious nor ponderously pleasant, but the periods marched forth in an ordered stream of words, punctuated in the process, so it seemed, by some invisible grammarian.

She flashed a dazzling smile at him which was partly thanks for her relief, partly amusement at his speech. The smile died as suddenly because of her amusement and her fear that he would realise why she smiled. (As to that she need not have worried, for Ted Talham had no fear of appearing ridiculous.)

"Perhaps you would allow me to see you safely from this place," he said courteously. "Civilisation has its dangers—dangers as multitudinous and as primitive as the wilds may hold for the innocent and the beautiful."

She flushed a little, but he was so obviously sincere, and so free from pretension, that she could not be offended.

"They have been following me for days," she replied. "At first I thought it was a coincidence, but now I see that there was no reason for their dogging my movements."

He nodded, and they walked on in silence for a while, then:

"Are you associated with China in any way?" he asked suddenly.

She smiled and shook her head.

"I have never been to China," she said, "and know very little about the country."

Again a silence.

"You have friends associated with China?" he persisted, and saw a little frown of annoyance gather on her forehead.

"My mother—that is to say, my stepmother has," she said shortly.

He curled his moustache thoughtfully. She noted with an odd feeling in which pleasure and annoyance were mixed, that he was very much "the old friend of the family." It was not exactly what he said, or the tone he adopted. It was an indefinable something which was neither patronage nor familiarity. It was Talham's way, as she was to discover, to come with pleasant violence into lives and be no more and no less in place than they who had won their positions in esteem and confidence through arduous years of service.

"Perhaps your mother's friends have given you something Chinese which these men want?" he suggested, and again saw the frown. Somehow he knew that it did not indicate hostility to, or annoyance with, himself.

"I have a bangle," she said; "but I do not wear it."

She stopped, opened a silver bag she carried on her wrist, and took out a small jade bracelet. It was set about at intervals by tiny bands of gold.

"May I see it?"

She passed it to him. They were nearing Marble Arch, and she had insensibly slackened her pace. Now they both stopped whilst he examined the ornament. He scrutinised it carefully. Between each band was an inscription, half obliterated by wear.

"This bangle is two thousand years old," he said simply, and she gasped.

"Two thousand!" she repeated incredulously.

"Two thousand," he repeated. "This is quite valuable."

"I know," she said shortly.

He detected something of resentment in her tone.

"What do those characters mean?" she asked. "Is it something I shouldn't know?" she asked quickly.

She looked up at his face. There was a dull flush on his face and a strange light in his eyes.

He fingered the jade bracelet absently.

"There is nothing you should not know," he said briefly—for him. "There is much that I have wanted to know for years."

She was puzzled, and showed it.

"Listen," he said, and read, turning the bracelet slowly as he read:

"I am Shun the son of the great mechanic Chu-Shun upon whom the door fell when the Emperor passed. This my father told me before the day, fearing the treachery of the eunuchs. Behold the pelican on the left wall with the bronze neck... afterwards the spirit steps of jade... afterwards river of silver, afterwards... door of bronze. Here Emperor... behind a great room filled with most precious treasures."

He read it twice, then handed the bracelet to the girl. She looked at him for the space of a minute. Here, in the heart of prosaic London, with the dull roar of the traffic coming to them gustily across the sparse herbage of a most commonplace park, Shun the son of Chu-Shun spoke across the gulf of twenty centuries.

"It is very wonderful," she said, and looked at the bracelet.

"I think you had better let me keep this bracelet," he said; "at any rate for a while. I beg you to believe"—he raised his hand solemnly—"that I consider only your own safety, and I am moved to the suggestion by the knowledge that you attach no sentimental value to the ornament, that it was given to you by somebody whom your mother likes, but who is repugnant to you, and that you only wear it in order to save yourself the discomfort and exasperation of a daily argument with your parent."

She stared at him in open-eyed amazement.

"How—how did you know that?" she asked.

"You carry it in your bag. You frowned when you took it out to show me," he said cheerfully. "You carry it in your bag only because you must keep it by you in order to slip it on and off when you are out of somebody's sight. If it were your fiancé, you would either wear it or leave it at home—engaged people clear up their differences as they go along. Evidently you are a lady of strong character, strong enough to respect the foibles or the demands of your elders. Therefore it must be your father or your mother; and since fathers are naturally indignant and notoriously unsentimental, I cannot imagine that he would insist——"

"Thank you," she said hurriedly. "Will you keep the bracelet for me, and return it at your leisure to this address?"

She extracted a card from her bag, and he looked at it and read:

MISS YVONNE YALE.
406, Upper Curzon Street, S.W.

"Yvonne," he read gravely. "I've never known anybody named Yvonne."

He put the bracelet in his inside pocket, and buttoned the worn coat again.

"I have no card," he said. "I am Captain Ted Talham of the Victorian Mounted Infantry, of the Bechuanaland Mounted Police, of the Imperial Bushmen, and I am, in addition, a general in the army of the Dowager Empress of China, a mandarin of the Fourth Class, and a wearer of the Sun of Heaven and the Imperial Dragon Orders."

He recited this with all gravity. There was no glint of humour in his eyes. The girl checked her smile when she realised how serious this good-looking man was. There was pride in the recital of his dignities: it was a very important matter that he should be Captain of Irregular Horse, and as tremendous a happening that he should wear the decorations of the Manchu dynasty.

She held out her hand.

"I am sure my mother will be glad to meet you," she said, "and as for myself I cannot tell you how grateful I am that you should have been so providentially at hand this afternoon."

He bowed, a ceremonious and correct little bow.

"That is the luck of the game," he said.

There was an awkward pause. He was so evidently trying to say something more.

"I think it is right, and it is my duty," he said at last, "to point out to you the very significant fact that so far I have not offered you my address. This," he went on oracularly, "is all the more significant and alarming when I tell you that the intrinsic value of the bangle"—he tapped his pocket—"is anything from fifteen hundred to twenty-five hundred pounds."

"Impossible!" said the startled girl.

It was altogether an amazing afternoon.

He nodded.

"Possibly the latter figure," he said. "Let the fact sink into your mind, and add to it the alarming intelligence that I have no address, and I have no address because I have exactly three yen in unchangeable Chinese silver between myself and the ravening world."

A wave of pity surged over the girl, and there were tears in her eyes—tears that sprang most unexpectedly from unsuspected wells of sympathy.

She fumbled in her bag, but he stopped her.

"I beg of you," he said reproachfully. "If you can't trust me with two thousand pounds' worth of jade, believe me, I can trust you with my secret, and a secret is only existent just so long as either of the two parties affected do nothing overtly or covertly to destroy the basic foundation upon which it rests. My secret is momentary penury—remove that and the secret ceases to be."

He would have said more, but checked himself.

"In fact," he concluded, "if you offer me money, I shall offer you your jade bangle, and there will be the end of the matter."

She was laughing now—her eyes danced with merriment.

There was something amusing in the situation. This seedy gentleman with his unchangeable yen, his problematical dinner and bed, with two thousand pounds in his inside pocket, appealed to her sense of the grotesque. If young De Costa knew! Young change-counting, bill-checking, tipless De Costa, who had given her two thousand pounds in the innocence of his heart.

"Promise me that you will call?" she asked laughingly, "with or without the bangle."

"With the bangle," he said. "To-night I shall make it very clear to the 'Noble Child,' 'Hope of the Spring,' and 'Star of the Yamen' that the bracelet has passed to my possession and that henceforward if they wish to follow its wearer they must follow me."

He shook hands again, lifted his hat, and turning abruptly, left her.

CHAPTER 2

THE MAN IN THE DRAWER

His Excellency Prince Chu-Hsi-Han, Ambassador to the Court of St. James, picked up the card from the tray, and examined it calmly through his rimless glasses.

"Is the distinguished stranger below?" he asked.

"Excellent Highness," said the Mongolian in the livery of the Embassy, "I placed the distinguished stranger in the red room."

The Ambassador nodded.

"Conduct him to my unworthy presence," he said, and the servant bowed twice and left the room silently.

He returned in a few minutes and announced the visitor in faultless English.

"Signor Tillizinni."

Tillizinni, spare of build, with his keen, eager face and his black and white colouring, formed a strong note in that room of soft pearl-blue draperies and shaded lights. He offered his hand with a little bow to the impassive Oriental who rose from his desk to meet him.

"Your Excellency expected me?" he asked, and the Ambassador smiled, for Tillizinni spoke in the Chinese—that peculiar "Mandarin Chinese" which only the statesmen and diplomatists of China employ.

"You are a veritable signor," he said quietly. "You have the accent which suggests a course of training in the forbidden city."

Tillizinni flushed—he was susceptible on the intellectual side.

"I am flattered," he said. "Yet I studied no nearer to Pekin than Florence."

"I congratulate you," said the Prince, and with his own hands drew a chair forward.

"Be seated," he said, "and tell me exactly what you require."

He was speaking in English now.

Tillizinni took from his pocket a long envelope and extracted a number of newspaper cuttings.

"Your Excellency wrote an article in the *North American Review*," he said, "which dealt extensively with the early history of your country."

The Ambassador nodded.

"You dealt extensively with the life of the First Emperor."

Again the Ambassador nodded.

"One could not deal effectively with the history of China," he smiled, "unless one wrote of the First Emperor. He built the great wall and stimulated all the best efforts of my countrymen—and though it was two thousand years ago, his influence is still felt."

It was Tillizinni who smiled now.

"His influence is felt here in London," he said grimly, "and in no place more completely than in Scotland Yard, which, as your Excellency may know, affords me employment."

"At Scotland Yard?"

The Chinese Ambassador's eyebrows rose.

"At Scotland Yard," repeated the other. "But if your Excellency will proceed——"

The Prince was a great littérateur, and since he was riding his hobby, needed little encouragement.

"The First Emperor did many wonderful things," he said. "He also did many things, which I say humbly and with due reverence to his illustrious memory"—he bowed his head—"were not wise, for he destroyed all the literature which China possessed, burnt books and documents, and forbade on pain of death any attempt on the part of students to retain the writings of the just. All this you will find dealt with in the story in a sketchy way."

Again Tillizinni nodded.

"Here is a paragraph I would like to direct your special attention," he said, and indicated a page on which a paragraph had been outlined with blue pencil.

"Pardon me!" said his Excellency. He was apologising for the fact that it was necessary for him to employ his pince-nez; for your well-bred Chinaman be he all but blind, does not wear his spectacles in the presence of his guest.

"Ah, that," he tapped the blue paragraph with his finger, "that is a literal extract from the writings of our greatest historian, and describes the burial of the First Emperor."

He read aloud in his soft English, tracing the printed lines with his tapered fingers as he proceeded:

"In the 9th moon the First Emperor was buried in Mount Li, which in the early days of his reign he had caused to be tunnelled and prepared with that view. Then, when he had consolidated the Empire, he employed his soldiery, to the number of 700,000, to bore down to the Three Springs (that is, until the water was reached), and there a firm foundation was laid and the sarcophagus placed thereon. Rare objects and costly jewels were collected from the palaces and from the various officials, and were carried thither and stored in huge quantities. Artificers were ordered to construct mechanical crossbows, which, if any one were to enter, would immediately discharge their arrows. With the aid of quicksilver, rivers were made—the Yangtsze, the Yellow River, and the great ocean—the metal being made to flow from one into the other by machinery. On the roof were delineated the constellations of the sky, on the floor the geographical divisions of the earth. Candles were made from the fat of the man-fish (walrus), calculated to last for a very long time. The Second Emperor said: 'It is not fitting that the concubines of my late father who are without children should leave him now'; and accordingly he ordered them to accompany the dead monarch to the next world, those who thus perished being many in number. When the interment was completed, some one suggested that the workmen who had made the machinery and concealed the treasure knew the great value of the latter, and that the secret would leak out. Therefore, so soon as the ceremony was over, and the path giving access to the sarcophagus had been blocked up at its innermost end, the outside gate at the entrance to this path was let fall, and the mausoleum was effectually closed, so that not one of the workmen escaped. Trees and grass were then planted around, that the spot might look like the rest of the mountain."

Tillizinni nodded.

"That is the trouble," he said.

"Trouble?"

It is not etiquette for a high-born Chinaman to express his astonishment in the exclamatory style of the West; yet the Prince was obviously astonished.

As briefly as possible Tillizinni gave a résumé of the events which had preceded and followed the stranding of the China mail-boat.

His Excellency listened, his features composed to that immobility which is characteristic of his race. When Tillizinni had concluded, he asked:

"You suggest that the thieves were seeking information which they knew I would publish, and which is to be found in every historical text-book on China."

"I suggest to your Excellency," said Tillizinni quietly, "that amongst your documents there was one which threw greater light upon the Treasure House of the Dead than anything you have published."

The Ambassador was silent. His delicate fingers played restlessly with a silver paper knife on his desk, and his eyes were averted from the other's face.

Tillizinni offered no encouragement to speech. He understood that he had been right in his surmise. There was reason for the attempted burglary and the reason was to be found in the contents of the mail-bag.

It was fully three minutes—no inconsiderable period of time—before the Ambassador spoke:

"I can only imagine," he said at last, speaking very slowly, "that the people who tried to rob the safe desired information which I am not prepared to give."

He looked up sharply.

"Do you realise, Mr. Tillizinni," he asked, "that buried with Ts'in Hwang Ti are jewels computed to be worth over two million pounds?"

"Two millions?"

The Prince nodded.

"Two millions," he repeated. "All the authorities agree that even in those days, China was enormously wealthy in gold and precious jewels, and that the value of the First Emperor's possessions were enormous. He was originally the King of Ts'in, and he it was who established the Empire. By conquest alone he must have secured enormous wealth apart from that which he obtained through the recognised revenues of peace."

The knowledge that this wealth lies buried is sufficient to tempt the foreign adventurer—no Chinaman save some of the worst criminal characters would desecrate a tomb.

"I have in my possession the exact location of Mount Li," he added simply.

"But——"

"You think that is easy to find, but as a matter of fact the Empire is filled with Mount Lis, and though on one of these—the most obvious one—the tomb has been located, the great Emperor is really buried on a small and barren island in the Gulf of Pe-chili."

Tillizinni's eyes narrowed.

What mystery there was in the burglary had now vanished.

"Why is not the location generally known?" he asked.

The Ambassador favoured him with one of his rare smiles.

"The Emperor himself forbade the disclosure," he said. "In China in those days, the Divine Sun of Heaven controlled not alone the destinies by the memories of men."

Tillizinni rose to go.

"One last question," he asked. "Do you intend publishing the information you have at any future date?"

"I do not," said the Ambassador briefly.

Tillizinni had occasion to go into the red drawing-room, where he had left his hat and walking-stick.

A man was sitting waiting—a tall, good-looking man, jaunty enough in spite of the poverty of his attire.

"Captain Talham, I believe," said Tillizinni, and the other rose.

"You are the gentleman who searched my luggage at King's Cross cloak-room," said Captain Talham, without resentment, and the detective laughed aloud.

"That is a confession which I should not care to make," he said. "How do you know your luggage had been searched?"

"I have had some experience," said the other coolly, "and it may interest you to know that, since your search, a more conscientious search-party took away the whole of my baggage and has, so far, failed to replace it."

Tillizinni was genuinely concerned. This strange man had a tender spot in his heart for the needy and it needed no second glance at the man from China to discover his straitened circumstances.

He drew a chair forward.

"I am interested in this," he said. "Perhaps I can help you."

Captain Talham raised a dignified and protesting hand.

"The normal mind," he said "rejects without hesitation the instinct of rebellion against recognised authority. Undisciplined resentment toward social safeguards imposed by society for its own protection is aluvistic. I appreciate the necessity for the examination you made and regard as admirable the choice of agent which the government has made. Moreover, since I am directly and frankly interested in discovering the location of Mount Li, and came to this country by the same ship as certain documents revealing that location, your suspicion was pardonable."

He said all this, scarcely pausing to take breath.

Tillizinni's face, schooled to conceal his emotion, displayed no hint of his sensations. Had this man been listening at the door of the study, that he should take up the threads of the Ambassador's discourse?

Talham seemed to divine the working of the Italian's mind, and smiled.

"I gather you have been discussing the matter with Chu-hsi-han. I gather that because you did not make your call till after the publication of his article, and because I have reason for knowing that that article has excited a great deal of interest in circles with which you are probably unacquainted—the Society of Good Intention, for example."

There was something in his tone which at once interested and nettled Tillizinni. The stranger had put him on his mettle, too, challenged his knowledge of forces. Yet the Italian was too big a man to allow pique to stand in his way of acquiring information. He was not too clever to learn.

"I know nothing whatever about the Society of Good Intention," he said; "though I gather from its benevolent title that it is a Chinese secret society with a felonious propaganda."

Talham was tickled. Here was a man after his own heart.

"The Society," he began, as if to deliver a speech, then changed his mind. "The Society is purely criminal, though it had a political origin. It is an off shoot of the Guild of Honourable Adventurers which flourished in Canton twenty years ago. It has committed more crimes than any other in China, and it has reached a pass where——"

Clear and sharp above the conversation a pistol shot rang out.

It sounded overhead, and simultaneously the two men leapt to their feet. With one accord they darted to the door, across the wide hall, and up the soft-carpeted stairs, Tillizinni leading, an automatic pistol in his hand.

A servant was standing at the door of the Ambassador's study, vainly twisting the handle.

"It is locked, Excellencies," he said.

"Out of the way!" cried Talham.

The man obeyed with suspicious alacrity. He flew down the stairs, past the chattering crowd of servants hurrying up.

At the door of the house the Chinaman in the livery of the Embassy was joined by another.

"We will go quickly, brother," said the first man, "else these people will know that we are not in the Tao-ae's service."

They passed through the door and out into the dark street as the sound of a crash told them that Talham had gained admission to the room above.

The room was in darkness, but the observant Tillizinni had noted the mother-of-pearl button switch, and his fingers found it now. Instantly the room was flooded with soft light.

Huddled in his chair was the Ambassador—dead.

There was no wound which the men could see, and Tillizinni, going swiftly to the side of the dead man, uttered an exclamation.

"He has been strangled!" he cried.

Talham leant over the desk, his brows puckered in a frown.

"Strangled! Then who fired that shot?" he asked.

Servants were coming into the room now. The English secretary pushed a way through a crowd of excited Chinamen. He had been writing in his study on the third floor when the shot aroused him.

"Marshall all the servants," said Tillizinni, and whilst this was being done the detective made an examination of the apartment. The windows were closed and fastened with a catch, for the Ambassador shared with his coun-trymen a horror of ventilation. There was no possibility of entry from that direction.

Nothing had been disturbed with the exception of a large inlaid bureau which stood against one wall of the room. Here the door had been wrenched open, and a drawer forced and ransacked. Private papers lay scattered on the floor.

Tillizinni picked up a large envelope. It was inscribed in Chinese characters: "The burial-place of the First Emperor." The seal on the envelope remained intact, but the cover had been slit from end to end, and was empty.

"Look!" said Talham's voice explosively.

Tillizinni followed the direction of the pointing finger. The bottom of the bureau was formed by one huge drawer, the width and depth of the massive piece of furniture and some eighteen inches high.

From one corner bright red drops were dripping and forming a little pool on the carpet.

The two men grasped the bronze handles of the drawer and pulled.

The body of a man lay in the bottom. He was doubled up so that his knees were under his chin. He had been shot evidently from behind, and was quite dead.

"Do you know him?" asked Tillizinni.

Talham nodded.

"He called himself the 'Star above the Yamen,'" he said, "and I had an interesting talk with him this afternoon."

For this poor, inanimate thing had been the spokesman of Hyde Park.

CHAPTER 3

INTRODUCES MR. SOO

It was a busy night for Captain Talham. The clocks were striking three when he hailed a taxi-cab. Tillizinni joined him as he stood on the edge of the pavement, and the two conversed together for some time. Then they entered a cab, and drove off.

The man who watched them from the opposite side of the road followed. His car waited in a side street at no great distance, and it was a car which readily overtook the cab which carried the two men eastward.

They passed through the stone archway of Scotland Yard, and the pursuing car continued its way along the Embankment, and in obedience to the instructions given through the speaking tube, slowed in Horse Guards Avenue to allow the occupant to alight.

He was dressed irreproachably in the evening dress of civilisation, and carried himself with ease and confidence. He walked back the way the car had come, turned into Scotland Yard without hesitation, and found the constable on duty very ready to carry a message to Tillizinni.

The Italian received him alone, and the visitor favoured him with a ceremonious bow.

Tillizinni took him in from foot to crown in one sweeping and comprehensive bow.

The newcomer was unquestionably Chinese, though he did not wear a *queue* which distinguished the Manchu before the rebellion. His face was good-looking for a Chinaman, his features clean-cut, his eyes alone betrayed his nationality. His lips, straight and thin, were expressionless, and Tillizinni noticed that this strange man, dressed in the height of fashion, yet with the restraint which marked the gentleman, wore in one eye a gold-rimmed monocle.

When he spoke there was no trace of a foreign accent.

"Mr. Tillizinni?" he said, and the other nodded. "My name is Soo—L'ang T'si Soo—and I am, as you may suppose, a compatriot of the unfortunate man who was murdered to-night."

Tillizinni nodded again.

"I know the Prince slightly," said Soo, as he seated himself, "and naturally I am distressed at the tragic news."

"News travels very fast," responded Tillizinni dryly. "The Ambassador has not been dead very long."

Soo inclined his head easily.

"I was passing the Embassy, and I saw a number of distracted servants—one of whom you sent to find a policeman," he explained. "Naturally the servants being commonplace Chinamen and inveterate gossips, were ready to talk to one of their race."

This was plausible enough. Tillizinni, at any rate, could find no fault with the explanation. He wondered why this Chinese exquisite should have sought him at three o'clock in the morning.

"It is very sad," continued L'ang T'si Soo, shaking his head, "that one so learned as his Excellency should have been cut off so ruthlessly."

"It is sadder to me," said Tillizinni, "that the 'Star above the Yamen' should also have been sacrificed."

What made him say this he could not understand. There was no reason at all why he should mention the second man.

The effect on his visitor was electrical. He rose instantly and noiselessly from his chair, the monocle dropped from his eye, and the eyelids lowered till the detective saw no more than two straight, glittering slits of black.

"'Star above the Yamen'?" he repeated. "What do you mean?"

All the suaveness, all the languid drawl had gone out of his voice: it was harsh and metallic. The white-gloved hands were clenched till the delicate kid was stretched to breaking point. He stood erect and tense; there was something animal in his poise, something tigerish in his attitude.

"What I mean," said Tillizinni slowly, "is just this. In addition to the Ambassador, a man was killed—shot from behind, evidently by his confederates. As I have reconstructed the crime, the murderers were disguised in the livery of the Embassy, and made their escape in the confusion. 'Star above the Yamen' was probably killed because his murderers desired something which he had. He has been identified by this."

The detective took a sheet of paper from his pocket, and handed it across the desk to the other.

Soo looked at the Chinese characters long and earnestly.

"It is copied from the man's *hong*, which was given to Captain Talham this afternoon by the man himself."

With a supreme effort T'si Soo recovered his self-possession. Without a word he handed back the sheet, fixed his eyeglass mechanically and relaxed into his chair.

"That is interesting," he said calmly. "Once I knew a 'Star above the Yamen,' but this is evidently another man. The characters change a little as between North and South China, and my friend does not use this *hong*."

Tillizinni's observant eye saw the tip of the visitor's tongue pass over the dry lips.

"Doubtless you wonder why I have come," said the Chinaman, "and it is only fair to you that I should explain who I am. Your companion——"

"My companion?" asked Tillizinni sharply.

"The gentleman who is waiting in the next room," said the suave Oriental, "until I have gone. His Excellency Ho-tao, which in our language means the River Mandarin, or as you would call him, Captain Talham, he would know me. I am the son of the Governor of T'si-lu: to all intents and purposes, I am the governor."

Tillizinni bowed.

He knew something of this man, who was educated at Oxford, rented the most expensive of Piccadilly flats, and was reputedly wealthy.

Soo rose to go.

"I am afraid I have allowed my curiosity and my natural interest in the fate of my countryman to trespass upon your time," he said. "Here is my address: if I can be of any assistance to you, please command me."

He put his card upon the table, and with a little bow, withdrew.

Three minutes later he was speeding eastward as fast as his car could go. He swept round from the Embankment to Blackfriars Bridge, and crossed the river. He alighted near the Borough.

"Wait for me!" he said briefly, and the muffled chauffeur answered in Cantonese.

In a tiny thoroughfare leading off Southwark Street were a number of small shops, shuttered and silent at this hour of the morning.

Soo tapped on the shutters of one. It was a gentle tattoo that he beat, yet the door which flanked the windows was instantly opened and he passed in. The shop was evidently a laundry, and a Chinese laundry at that. He passed swiftly across the shop through the living-room at the back, in which one feeble light burned, and without hesitation turned sharply and descended the stairs which led directly from the living-room to the cellars below.

At the bottom of the stairs was a door. Again he knocked, and again the door was opened by a Chinaman in his shirt-sleeves.

The man removed his pipe as Soo entered, and made a profound obeisance.

The cellar was a large one, and its walls were covered with blood-red paper on which were painted crude, black drawings and characters illustrating the "Song of Lament." There was one table above which an oil-lamp swung, and about were seated half a dozen men in various conditions of dishabille.

Despite the coldness of the night, the cellar was uncomfortably hot, for a big charcoal brazier glowed in a wall recess where in some forgotten age had stood a European stove.

The men rose as Soo entered, concealing their hands in their sleeves.

"Where is my brother?" asked Soo quickly.

He addressed a cadaverous old Chinaman who stood nearest the brazier.

"Lord," said the man, "your illustrious brother has not returned."

"Where are Yung-ti and Hop-lee?" demanded Soo.

"Lord, they have not returned," answered the other.

Soo looked at his watch.

"Ming-ya says——" began the old man, but stopped as if he thought better of it.

"Ming-ya says—what?" asked Soo. "Answer me, old fool, quickly!"

The old man bowed.

"The seven blessings of heaven upon your highness," he said humbly. "But Ming-ya says that neither Yung-ti nor Hop-lee will return."

Ming-ya, a youthful Cantonese with the dull eye of an opium sot, nodded.

"That is true," he croaked hoarsely; "for these two men I heard speaking to-night when I was taking my pipe, and they thought I could not hear them—they go to China to-night."

Soo waited for a time; his head sank on his chest, buried in thought.

Then his eye singled out a thoughtful face which had been turned to him from the moment he entered. It was the face of a young man who stood where the shadow of the lamp fell—for one side of the lamp had been shaded so that no gleam of direct light could be detected from the street above. With a jerk of his head Soo signed for him to follow, and without another word the two men left the cellar, the door closing behind them with a click.

In the shop above T'si Soo turned to his companion.

"Lo-Rang," he said, "these two men have killed my brother—and yours, for we of the Society of Good Intention are all brothers, having sworn by our ancestors to keep faith. Also they have taken away a certain paper which I sent them to get."

The younger man inclined his head obediently.

"I sent my brother with them because I feared treachery. He it was—so the foreigners say—who found the paper, and because they needed it for their treachery and could get it no other way, they have killed him."

"Excellency," said Lo-Rang meekly, "all this I know. Tell me what I shall do?"

"Find those men," said Soo, "and *shah!*"

The young man bowed reverently and turned, disappearing into the back of the shop.

He returned with a tiny bundle of clothes, and a long, narrow-bladed knife.

"This is the knife with which I killed a man in Hoo Sin," he said proudly, and Soo nodded his acknowledgment.

CHAPTER 4

THE AMULET OF JADE

MR. RAYMOND DE COSTA put down his paper, and looked thoughtfully at his son who sat opposite to him at the breakfast-table.

Gregory de Costa favoured his father in that he was below the medium height and somewhat stout for a man of twenty-four. His complexion had a tinge of bronze-red, which is to be found in those families which trace back to "colour," and, indeed, there was a history of a mésalliance which brought wealth but an undesirable Eurasian strain into the De Costa family. They referred to themselves as a Portuguese house, and Portuguese they may have been originally; but generations of De Costas had lived and died in the Madras presidency, illustrious amongst the chee-chee folk, but unquestionably of them.

Raymond, the elder, was the richest of the De Costa clan. He was fat and wheezy; his face was swollen with good living and self-indulgence—for he denied himself none of the excellencies of life. It was not an attractive face, though the two black eyes that burned all the time as though with fever, were fascinating. They were "seeing" eyes; they watched and absorbed all things within their radius. They were terribly alive and eager. They seemed to denote and indicate a separate existence to that which the gross, unshapely body of the man enjoyed.

The elder man—he must have been sixty—raised his be-ringed hand and gently caressed the stubble of grey moustache on his upper lip.

He was contemplating this dreadful son of his, from his sleek, shiny head, to his sleek, shiny boots.

"Gregory," he said after a while, "have you seen the papers this morning?"

The younger man shook his head.

"No," he admitted, though in the admission he knew he might earn a reproof, for he was undergoing a course of education which included a knowledge of the daily happenings of life.

To his surprise the inevitable lecture was not forthcoming. Instead——

"The Chinese Ambassador was murdered last night," said his father softly.

Gregory stared.

There was something in the very gentleness of Raymond de Costa's voice which made the younger man feel uncomfortable.

"Murdered—poor devil!" he said. "Was that where you went last night? I suppose they sent for you?"

Raymond sat upright suddenly.

"Where I went! What do you mean?" he demanded harshly. "I went nowhere."

"I thought I heard you come in at one o'clock," said the youth, reaching for an apple from the table. "I didn't sleep too well."

The other frowned.

"I did not come in for an excellent reason," he said with asperity; "I was in bed at eleven o'clock and I did not stir out of my bed until Thomas brought my coffee this morning."

The young man was unconvinced.

"But, governor," he protested, "I saw Thomas with your boots, and they were all covered with mud."

The old man thumped the table with a snarl of anger.

"I wasn't out of the house last night, I tell you!"

Gregory de Costa was alarmed at the storm he had brought down upon his head.

"I'm sorry," he mumbled apologetically. "I must have dreamt it."

"What is this about you're not sleeping well?" demanded the other, changing the conversation abruptly. "Are you ill?"

"Ill? No; it's nothing! I'm just feeling a bit rotten."

He got up from the table and walked disconsolately to the window, gazing gloomily into the street.

"Is it that girl of yours?" asked his father with a slight smile.

"Which girl?" asked the other resentfully "Do you mean Miss Yale?"

"Who else?"

The youth was silent for a while.

"She's not my girl by any means, governor," he said despairingly. "I wish to heaven she was! She treats me like dirt—absolutely like dirt!"

Raymond de Costa smiled.

"Pretty people to treat a son of mine like dirt," he said disdainfully. "The mother is head over heels in debt; the girl only looks presentable because she does a little writing. Why don't you make up to the mother?"

The young man turned round, his hands thrust deep into his trouser pockets, discontent eloquently written on his face.

"The mother's all right," he grumbled. "I can twist Mrs. Yale round that." He held up a stodgy little finger. "If it was only the mother there would be no trouble. It's the girl."

"Give her presents; women like that sort of thing!" suggested his father, but the young man shook his head.

"I've given her——" He stopped.

"What?"

"Oh, lots of things!" said the youth vaguely. His conscience was troubling him a little. Something was very much on his mind.

There is an intense sympathy between some fathers and some sons which is generally all to the good. It sometimes, however, works out to the embarrassment of one of the partners. De Costa *père* had a trick of catching mind impressions; and now there came to him the recollections of something he wished to say.

"By the way," he said carelessly, "Miss Yale has something which I should very much like to possess."

The youth made no attempt to discover what that something was. He glanced a little apprehensively at his parent and waited.

"Miss Yale," the other went on, "has a bangle, which, from the description I have had of it, must be the very companion of one which I have been scouring the world to secure, and which that thief Song-lu of Nanping swore he had dispatched to me by registered post."

He rose from the table too, a scowl on his unpleasant face.

"It cost me over a thousand pounds to find, and another thousand to buy," he said; "and Song-lu expects me to believe that he entrusted it to the registered post!"

"When ought it to have arrived?" stammered Gregory, very red in the face and horribly conscious of a desire to bolt.

"During my absence in China," said his father. Then, sharply: "You saw nothing of a bangle, did you?"

Gregory de Costa cleared his throat.

"I wanted to say—I've had an uncomfortable feeling," he said incoherently, "that a bangle came to me—at least I thought it was for me—some old curio that you'd picked up, governor. I hadn't any idea it was for you; it was just addressed 'Mister de Costa'."

"Ah, you've got it!" There was relief and pleasure in Raymond de Costa's face.

The son hesitated.

"Well," he said, "I haven't exactly got it. As a matter of fact I thought you meant me to give it away—so I gave it!"

De Costa stared at his son open-mouthed. His face went paler and paler with almost unconquerable rage.

"Gave it away?" he said at last, restraining himself with the greatest effort. "And to whom did you give it, you precious fool?"

"I gave it to Miss Yale," said the young man sullenly. "How was I to know?"

"How was he to know?" De Costa, senior, appealed to the ceiling in his exasperation. "How was he to know that I should not waste my time picking up curios for a moon-calf? Oh, Gregory Marcus de Costa, you make me tire!"

It was chee-chee now. All the Eurasian in him was indicated in his voice and his manner. Tears of rage stood in his eyes.

Only a man of iron will could have overcome his natural disabilities as did old De Costa, because of a sudden he became very calm.

"You must go at once to Miss Yale, and on any excuse whatever you must regain possession of that bracelet. Tell her," he bent his brows in thought, "tell her that you have learnt that it came from somebody who was suffering with the plague. Tell her anything—but get the bangle. She shall have diamonds in its stead. Go!"

"I'm awfully sorry, governor," began Gregory.

The old man bared his teeth.

"Get out!" he said savagely.

Gregory de Costa went to his room with a grievance and a fear. Suppose Yvonne Yale would not surrender this precious circle of jade? Suppose she were hurt—no such luck! The worst and the most likely thing that could happen would be that she would seize an excellent and providential opportunity for ridding herself of an undesirable suitor.

He dressed himself with care, swearing at his reflection in the glass as at his worst enemy. He counted his money mechanically before transferring it from one pocket to the other—a frugal soul was Gregory de Costa!—and examined with care the interior of his pocket-book. He would avail himself of his father's offer. It would be a diamond bracelet which he would offer as a substitute, and no girl in her senses could refuse that. He found consolation in the prospect, and finished his dressing carefully.

The Yales, mother and daughter, lived in a tiny house in Upper Curzon Street—a little house which had managed to squeeze itself between two more imposing façades and strove unsuccessfully to pretend that it had been there all the time.

Miss Yale was alone, the servant informed him, and added with the garrulous familiarity of a servant from whom her mistress had no secrets, that she had gone to the bank.

In the little drawing-room on the first floor Mr. de Costa junior found a lady who was coldly polite and undisguisedly surprised to see him at that hour in the morning.

He blundered to his fate.

"Fact is, Miss Yvonne——" he began.

"Miss Yale," she corrected him with a little smile.

"Sorry. Fact is, there's been a plague."

"A plague?"

He nodded vigorously, satisfied with the sensation he had created.

"But I'm afraid that I don't understand," she said. "Where is the plague, and what has it to do with me?"

"In China," he lied glibly. "Thousands of fellows dead. My governor is awfully upset; that bracelet, you know."

She began to comprehend, and nodded.

"You see," he went on eagerly, "the man that owned it has the plague, and the governor's awfully concerned about you. So if you'll let me have it, we'll just put it where it can do no harm."

He was flushed with self-satisfaction; already it seemed his task was satisfactorily performed. But her next words sent a flood of ice-water down his back.

"I'm sorry," she said; "but I haven't got it."

"Haven't? Oh, I say, Miss Yvonne! Oh, come now!" he almost wailed. "You must have it. I shall get into an awful row!"

"I am sorry you will get into trouble," she said quietly; "but I haven't got it at the moment."

"But you must have it, Miss—Miss Yale. You must!" He was violent almost in his terror at facing his father empty-handed. "And I must insist upon your giving it to me."

A wrong—a fatally wrong—move on the part of Gregory de Costa.

The girl stood up, stiff and uncompromising.

"You insist?" she said scornfully. "You forget that the bracelet is mine, though I assure you I've no desire to keep it. In a short time I shall have it, and it will be sent to you. Good morning!"

"If I've said anything offensive," pleaded the young man humbly, yet in his humility mopping his brow with a handkerchief, the gaudiness of which was in itself an offence.

"Good morning!" said Yvonne Yale, with a little inclination of dismissal.

There was a knock at the door, and De Costa checked his flood of apology.

"Captain Talham," announced the servant, and Captain Talham followed her quickly into the room.

The girl flashed a little smile of welcome, then turned to the young man.

"Captain Talham will give you what you desire," she said coldly; then, to the tall man: "Will you please give this gentleman the bracelet I gave you yesterday?"

Talham looked from the girl to the youth, and from the youth to the girl. Then, with a sigh in which relief was evident, he drew from his right hand pocket something wrapped in tissue paper and placed it in the outstretched hand of the other.

"Phew!" said Mr. Gregory de Costa, and unwrapped the jade bracelet set about with bands of gold. "Phew!" he said again, and his trembling fingers stowed the precious circlet in an inside pocket.

Captain Talham scrutinised him gravely.

"My friend," he said, "on what small and seemingly trivial incident does life turn! A petulant word—the hint of offensiveness to this dear lady"—he waved his hand gracefully in the direction of the embarrassed Yvonne—"a sudden revulsion of feeling, which turns penitence to stern and unscrupulous purpose, hardens the shamed heart, and adds lustre to villainy."

"I beg your pardon?" asked young Mr. de Costa reasonably puzzled.

Talham would have proceeded, but something in the girl's eyes, some mute entreaty, averted him. He favoured the young man with a bow which effectively dismissed him and turned his attention to the girl.

She waited until the door closed behind him.

"You are always getting me out of scrapes, Captain Talham," she smiled.

"You've got me out of a scrape," he said solemnly, and seated himself at her gesture.

He had been up all night, he told her without invitation.

He added that he had borrowed a sovereign from a famous detective whom, with unnecessary caution, he described as Signor T——.

"Not that I've been to sleep," he said. "I have been engaged with a Chink"—he saw she was puzzled—"a Chinaman," he hastened to correct himself. "A very admirable man, who does things."

An ambiguous but characteristic description, she thought.

He was ill at ease, and remarkably silent through the interview; spoke little, yet several times seemed to be on the point of speaking.

"You seem to have something to confess," she said at last in gentle raillery.

She had to make conversation at an hour of the day when small talk was a most difficult exercise to assume, and was at her wits' end for subjects.

Three times he had started with an ominous "I feel that I ought to tell you"; and three times he had stopped and talked rapidly for a minute or two about some subject wholly irrelevant to the matter under discussion.

"I have and I haven't," he said slowly. "That is to say, I had, and probably that from a strictly ethical standpoint still have. It is a nice question."

He rose to go with startling abruptness.

"There is something troubling you, my man," thought she in an amused way.

"Miss Yale," he said solemnly. "In war all expedients are justified."

"I agree," she smiled. "But exactly what are you thinking about?"

It may be that Captain Talham had no intention of telling her at that precise moment. What is certain, however, is that in his agitation he pulled his handkerchief from an inside pocket and with it something which fell upon the floor.

The girl looked at it in wonder; and well she might, for there was an absolute replica of the ornament she had returned to young De Costa a few moments before.

CHAPTER 5

MR. SOO MAKES A DISCOVERY

MR. DE COSTA, senior, sat in his study until late that night. His son had gone to a musical comedy to the relief of his mind and the repair of a crushed spirit, and Mr. de Costa was alone in the house save one man-servant—a half-caste factotum, who was neither butler nor errand-boy nor valet, and yet performed the functions of each.

At nine o'clock a man came to the house and was admitted through the servants' entrance. He was shown at once to the study.

De Costa looked over his glasses at the visitor and pointed to a chair.

"Sit down, Soo," he said, and the Chinaman, with a jerk and wriggle intended to display his respect for superiority, and his reluctance to seat himself in the presence of greatness, obeyed.

He was above medium height, and pallid even for a Chinaman. His high cheekbones and thin, straight lips, gave him sinister appearance, yet he was by no means bad-looking, for the nose was straight and well proportioned to the face. He wore no *queue*, and his black hair was brushed back in the style affected by the youth of England. His eyes were larger than the average, set about in a void face—void of emotion, of the expression and capacity for feeling.

Whatever humility convention may have dictated on his arrival, he had no false views on the question of his equality for the man who sat at the desk, for he leant over, lifted the lid of a silver box, and extracted a cigarette.

"Well," asked Mr. de Costa, blotting a letter he had written, "what is the news?"

The man he called Soo shook his head as he applied a light to the cigarette.

"I come to you for news," he said. "In my humble circle we talk of nothing more interesting than the surprising results which follow a game of Fan-tan."

"Where did you pick up your English?" asked De Costa irritably. It is never pleasant to know that one whom in your heart you grade below your own intellectual level is your superior in scholastic attainments.

"I picked it up in the place where one acquires much enlightenment," said Soo carelessly.

He blew a ring of smoke towards the ceiling, and watched it disappear.

"You wouldn't imagine," said he, "that I was intended for the ministry; yet that is the fact. There were good people who thought I would make an ideal missionary, and by the force of my personality and the knowledge of my own people, wean them from the traditions and the philosophies of two thousand years to the half-hearted philosophies, imperfectly understood and imperfectly promulgated in twenty different ways by the intelligent people of this country."

De Costa said nothing. He was too wily a man to be drawn into a discussion on a subject with which he was not too well acquainted.

Soo had an irritating trick of getting him out of his depths.

"I understand you've got the bracelet," said the Chinaman, and the other acknowledged the possession.

He unlocked the drawer of his desk, and took out a steel box. From this he extracted the bangle which Talham had handed to his son.

It was still in its paper wrapping, and Soo paused awhile before he removed the tissue.

"It is very light for jade," he said suspiciously.

He threw the end of his cigarette into the fireplace with a quick movement of his hand, and stripped the ornament of its wrapper.

He looked at it carefully, twisting the bangle about in his hand.

"This is not jade," he said.

"Not jade," repeated the merchant, and half rose from his chair. "Are you sure?"

"This is celluloid," said the calm Soo, "cleverly copied and possibly weighted to give it the appearance of jade."

He balanced it carefully on his hand; then he examined the gold bands.

"Yes, as I thought," he said, "the weight is in the gold."

He inspected the inscriptions and read them carefully. Half obliterated as they were, it was no easy task to decipher them by artificial light. Then he put the bangle upon the table.

"Your friend has deceived you," he said quietly. "This is not the famous Shu Shun bracelet. It is not even an imitation. These writings"—he tapped the bangle with his fingers—"are commonplace copybook maxims, as you would call them in this country."

He picked up the ornament again, and read: "An ungrateful son is a disappointed father." "The father of patience is wisdom, and the source of peace is love."

"You have been fooled, my friend!" he said.

De Costa sprang to his feet.

"Explain what you mean," he said.

The Chinaman was lighting another cigarette.

"It is very simple." He looked abstractedly at the ceiling, and spoke half to himself: "The girl had the original bracelet, and has returned this. Either she, or one of her friends, has the bangle; and it is our business to get it. Without that"—he lowered his voice—"everything that happened yesterday was in vain."

"Don't talk about yesterday," said De Costa hurriedly. "That is a subject which I never wish to discuss; you don't know how I'm feeling about it, Soo. I never wanted anybody hurt, I swear I didn't."

The Chinaman interrupted him with a slow smile.

"These things are not done by politeness," he said. "You are going into a big enterprise, and you must take a correspondingly big risk."

"I take no risks," said De Costa, white of face. "I know nothing whatever about it. Two deaths! My God, they couldn't——"

Soo nodded.

"They could indeed," he said easily. "If anybody hangs for what happened last night, be sure that you hang with them. You have gone into this matter, De Costa, with your eyes open. You saw a chance of obtaining an enormous treasure, and you took all risk. You Westerners," he went on, "place too high a value upon human life."

He half rose from his chair, leant across to the desk, and picked up the bangle again, examining it with an amused smile. Then, as he replaced it upon the table, he said grimly: "The events of yesterday about which you do not wish to speak, would have been wholly unnecessary had I known in time that this bangle existed."

"But surely," began De Costa, "the paper you found——"

Soo shook his head. He was calmness itself. "I have no papers," he said simply.

De Costa stared at him.

"No papers! What do you mean?"

"I mean exactly what I say," said the other. He marked the situation upon the outstretched fingers of his hand. "Three men were sent to secure an envelope from the Chinese Ambassador's bureau, and one of them was killed. Two made their escape with the papers concerning the matter. I have not seen them since."

"Gone?" said De Costa.

"Gone!" repeated the other. "There is another influence at work. I am inclined to associate an old acquaintance of mine—Captain Talham. You probably know him!"

De Costa nodded.

"He is interested in this matter of Mount Li. So firm was my conviction that he was behind the treachery of my two men, that I took the liberty of preparing a little surprise for him last night. Unfortunately," he said with regret, "it did not materialise. But to-night—who knows?"

He rose abruptly, and buttoned his overcoat, turning up the collar about his neck.

"I must go now," he said. "There is a lot of work to be done before to-morrow morning."

"What work?" asked De Costa.

"I am going to recover the bracelet," said Soo, and there was that in his eyes which made the older man quail.

"There will be no violence?" he stammered.

"None, I assure you," said the other airily.

"Remember," said De Costa almost tremulously, "that it is a woman you have to deal with."

"I have dealt with many women," said Soo, "and I find very little difference between the sexes save that the gentler is a trifle more courageous, and a little more willing to bear the consequences of their folly."

De Costa accompanied him into the regions of the kitchen and showed him to the door which led to the area. Not another word was spoken between the two men.

De Costa closed the door behind his visitor and bolted it securely. He went back to his study and drained off a glass of neat brandy.

He went to bed that night in no happy frame of mind.

He might have been less happy, as he lay tossing from side to side in his bed, had he seen the dark figure of a man stealing in the shadow of the wall which formed a tiny courtyard at the back of his house.

CHAPTER 6

A CRIME OF TILLIZINNI

WHOEVER the masked man was who was working so deliberately at the back door of Mr. de Costa's respectable dwelling, he went to work methodically and without any indication that he feared detection. He carried a little tiny kit of tools which he had spread upon the ground, and from time to time he leant down and selected one of these by the light of a small electric lamp which he flashed for a moment upon the kit's contents.

He took some trouble to avoid anything in the nature of a violent noise, and it was half an hour before the lock, and a portion of the door, came away very gently in his hand.

As methodically he leant down and rolled up the tools, placing them in his pocket; he pushed the door open, and entered.

He had no difficulty in forcing another door, or in gaining the wide hall-way which formed the principal entrance to the house.

In half an hour he pursued his inquiries with quiet confidence.

The dining-room yielded nothing; the rather ornate drawing-room no more. Yet he made a systematic search, flickering his light here and there, moving such pictures as he thought might conceal that which he sought.

He reserved his examination of the study till the last. He found some cigarette ends in the fireplace and picked them up cautiously, examining the brand with the light of his lantern. These he wrapped carefully in a piece of paper, and placed in his waistcoat pocket. He opened all the drawers and methodically examined them, replacing them just as he had found them, and relocked the drawers after him with a curious key which he took from his pocket.

After a while he mounted the stairs.

De Costa occupied the first room on the second floor, and the door faced the stairs, and on the right was another door, which led to the dressing-room, which again gave access to the principal bedroom.

The visitor made no attempt to force the door for some minutes, but devoted his attention to the door on the right.

It opened easily. He stood in the doorway listening. For all he knew De Costa may have had alarms fixed; but no bell or buzzer woke the stillness of the night. He closed the door gently behind him; the floor was carpeted with thick felt, and the precaution he had taken of enclosing his feet in goloshes was unnecessary. In this room, as he knew, was the intimate safe of the merchant's.

He had come prepared to open that safe and inspect its interior. In his pocket was a heavy iron bottle containing sufficient oxygen for his purpose, and in another pocket the blow-pipe and the instruments necessary to burn out the lock of the safe.

He switched on his pocket light, and turned it unhesitatingly in the direction of where the safe was to be found. Instantly his thumb closed upon the switch, and his light went out. Facing him was a man who stood with his back to the safe. His face was covered with a black crêpe mask, and in his hand, pointing insistently in the direction of the other, was a long-barrelled Colt revolver.

He might have saved himself the trouble of switching off his light, for instantly from the stranger's disengaged hand a white beam of light shot out. He had come similarly equipped.

"Go downstairs," whispered the man by the safe, "and keep your hands away from your pockets."

There was nothing for the burglar to do but to obey. Without a word he turned and walked out of the room, the other following a few paces behind.

"To the kitchen!" whispered the second man, and the burglar turned obediently.

They entered the big, underground kitchen together, the second man closing the door behind him before he felt on the wall for the switch. In a minute the room was illuminated, and they stood facing each other.

"Who are you?" asked the second man quietly.

"I prefer to remain anonymous," said the burglar.

He was the taller of the two, a man above medium height, and his voice had just that touch of culture which one does not expect from a member of the criminal classes.

"I prefer to see your face," said the second man.

The burglar shrugged his shoulders.

"Existence," he said oracularly, "is made up of unsatisfied desires. Nature in the ordering of her plans does not take into account the prejudices——"

"Good heavens!" gasped the other. "Captain Talham!"

The burglar was silenced momentarily, apparently annoyed too.

"I am Captain Talham," he said with ridiculous pride, and took off his mask; "though why you should know me I fail to understand."

The second man laughed—a low, musical, chuckling laugh.

"I know you all right," he answered.

Talham stood for a moment fidgeting by the side of the kitchen table; then:

"Let us put our cards on the table, Tillizinni," he said.

It was the second man's turn to start.

"Oh, yes, I know you!" Talham went on. "I always remember people by their hands; and as you probably know, the third knuckle of your left is more prominent than any other."

Tillizinni laughed.

"We seem to have made a pretty mess of it between us," he said; "as I gather, we are both here on the same errand."

Talham nodded.

"You can save yourself the trouble of tampering with the safe. I've already been to it."

"How did you get in?" asked Talham.

The detective shook his head with a smile.

"The last thing I can do is to arrange to get out," he answered evasively. "What did you find?"

Talham hesitated.

"I found nothing, save that our friend T'si Soo has been here. Some of his cigarette ends were in the fireplace; at least, they are Chinese, and I gather——"

Tillizinni nodded.

"I didn't need his cigarette ends to know that," he said. "I saw him come out."

They left the house together, walking arm in arm, through the front door, leaving the door ajar, and walked away under the very nose of a policeman who stood at the corner of a street a hundred yards from the house.

For a long time neither man spoke. Then Tillizinni burst into a fit of uncontrollable laughter.

"You amuse me very much," he said, "although you annoy me. Here is a situation worthy of a comic opera. I go to burgle a house for my own private ends. I meet another burglar, whom it is my duty, as an officer of the law, to arrest."

"Let's go and talk it over!" said Talham.

* * * *

"You're a curious man," said Tillizinni, and Captain Talham did not consider it worth while to correct him, though "curious" was an obvious misapplication of a word.

A bright, cheerful fire burnt in the big Adams' fireplace, and the shaded lamp on the table afforded enough light to the room. Outside, day was breaking over the dull silver of the river and slow moving tugs were passing up with the tide, drawing a trail of clumsy barges in their wake.

Tillizinni's rooms in Adelphi Terrace offered the finest view in London, but never was London more attractive than in the early hours of a frosty winter morning.

Neither of the two men had slept that night. A bundle of papers, each giving a brief account of the tragedy, was at the detective's elbow. He looked across to Talham in his worn garments. You could not pity the tall man. His confidence, his self-satisfaction—in the best sense of the word—precluded pity. He sat now with a fragrant cigar between his teeth, a steaming cup of coffee within reach on a little table by his side, his legs crossed—a model of contentment.

"I gather, of course," Tillizinni went on, "that you wanted to find the Ts'in tomb, and I must confess that I regarded your search as being little removed, in point of self-interest, from the efforts of our Chinese friends."

Talham shook his head.

"Accustomed as you are to the venal predilections——" he began.

Tillizinni put up his hands to his ears in mock despair.

"Do you forget that I am Italian?" he asked.

The great anthropologist was a man of quick likes and quicker dislikes. Never before had he found one to whom he felt so warm and so instant a regard as he did with this adventurer. Add the warm and generous qualities of his southern nature, interest in the *rara humanis* which his science dictated, and there is every excuse for the sudden friendship which has so often been the subject of criticism.

Tillizinni was at the zenith of his fame; he had handled the danger of the Fourth Plague with rare courage and ingenuity, and his name at this time was in all mouths. Even Scotland Yard, a cautious institution which does not take the stranger to its bosom, however brilliant he may be, had succumbed to his fascination, and Room 673E was "Mr. Tillizinni's Room," just as surely and unalterably as Room 1 is the Chief Commissioner's.

He leant forward to stir the fire, and to return an escaping coal to its glowing inferno.

"Will your man do the work you require?" he asked.

"In the time?"

The detective nodded, and Talham pursed his lips thoughtfully.

"He has till eleven," he said; "and a Chinese mechanic can do much in seven hours."

There was a restful little interval of silence, which Tillizinni broke.

"It is most fantastic—the most bizarre idea I have ever heard," he said. "From no other human being in the world would I accept such a story. Yet I believe you."

"Of course you do," retorted Talham simply.

Tillizinni stared; then an amused smile crossed his thin lips. The other surveyed him with great earnestness, then leant forward.

"Signor Tillizinni," he said, "the acquirement of wealth is a process which too often dissipates the qualities of self-respect. I will be a millionaire, not as the thief who robbed a tomb of dross"—he snapped his fingers finely—"but as the genius who wrested from the dead ages the secret and its attainments. I am satisfied that in the tomb of Ts'in I shall have revealed to me that supreme mechanical wonder of all time—perpetual motion."

His face was tense; his eyes glossed with the splendour of the thought. So the eyes of Christopher Columbus might have burnt as he sighted, through the spray, the low, grey cloud of land upon his bow.

"All this story of mechanical devices," Talham went on rapidly. "These rivers of quicksilver which run for ever by some complexity of machinery—it is all true. There may be little or no treasure; but that device lies hidden as surely as the bones of the architects are upon the floor of the chasm."

He rose, and paced the room with short, quick, nervous steps.

"But suppose when you opened the tomb you found nothing?" asked Tillizinni. "Suppose the device was non-existent and the quicksilver rivers had disappeared, and there was nothing but the store of treasure?"

Talham thought for a while.

"I should take the treasure," he said impressively, "and afterwards I should close the tomb reverently and come away."

Tillizinni laughed. It was a long, rich, chuckling laugh of pure enjoyment, which not even the reproachful eye of the other could suppress.

"I like you," said Tillizinni; "and if I do not consider it my duty to hamper you, I shall find a pleasure in helping you in your search."

Ten minutes later, the two men were dozing in their chairs, proof enough of the ease which comes with friendship.

It was not until ten o'clock, with the bright, winter's sunlight flooding the room, that Tillizinni awoke with a sense of refreshment. The big lamp upon the table still burnt, and he extinguished it.

His eyes fell upon Talham still fast asleep. His legs outstretched, his hands thrust into trouser pockets, and his chin on his breast.

Tillizinni moved across the room noiselessly, and looked out into the terrace below. There were two tradesmen's carts delivering goods at a neighbouring club. He closed the French windows of the room and returned to Talham, and dropped his hand upon the other's shoulder.

Talham was awake instantly.

"Anything wrong?" he asked, as he saw the other's face.

Tillizinni shook his head.

"That we are both alive is evidence that nothing is wrong," he said. "Look at the mantelpiece!"

Talham raised his eyes.

On the shelf above the fireplace, between two Tanagra statuettes, was a small, square, black box, as large as a small tea-caddy, and not unlike one in its appearance. Dependent from the case, hung a length of fuse some eight inches long, and the end was burnt black.

"Ashes in the fireplace—obviously fuse," said Tillizinni, kneeling down. "What made it stop burning, I wonder?"

He examined the little rope minutely, using a reading-glass.

"That's blood!" He pointed with his finger to a stain near the burnt end. "The man who placed this here had blood on his hands—probably cut himself in making the entrance. Now, where?"

He walked to the door of the room and, opening it, crossed the broad landing. Another room opened from here, and he entered. It was used as a box-room, and should have been locked. For the matter of that, it should have possessed a lock of more service than the twisted piece of metal that lay on the floor.

"Wrenched off with a modern pocket-jack," said Tillizinni approvingly. "A neat piece of work. Don't touch the lock; we'll hunt for a finger-print by and by. Window open! Humph!"

It was clear which way the thing had come.

"We've had a narrow escape," said Tillizinni.

"So did he," said Talham.

CHAPTER 7

AN AFTERNOON CALL

TALHAM was seized with the idea of making an afternoon call, and waited on Tillizinni, to the detective's embarrassment.

"Tillizinni," he said, "one of the duties which civilisation imposes upon its products, is the obligation under which we all rest, to observe the social amenities."

After which preamble he deigned to explain that he had accepted an invitation for himself and for the detective, to what he termed "a party."

Tillizinni had visions of being called upon to sing, or do parlour tricks, and he hastily excused himself.

"You must come," said Talham gravely. "I did perhaps overstep the conventions when, without consulting you, I accepted this invitation on your behalf. But I think you will enjoy yourself. Mrs. Smith is a lady of singular charm of manner, and has the gift which so few women, and indeed so few men, possess, of appreciating scientific endeavour at its true value."

From which Tillizinni gathered that the lady had been engaged in impressing upon Talham what a fine fellow he was.

The detective hesitated. He knew he would be horribly bored, but it must be confessed he was possessed by a curiosity to know exactly how Talham would behave in that nebulous sphere which is called "society."

Mrs. Smith had a little house in Bayswater. It was in one of those long roads which connect Bayswater with Mayfair, and where, at the Mayfair end, the houses grow narrower and narrower, crowding against one another as if in a panic lest they stray into the more unfashionable end of the street.

She was a woman who had a passion for parties, and was never quite so happy as when she was making two guests groan where one had groaned before.

Since her entertaining area was severely restricted, it is not to be wondered that her little social plot was somewhat overcrowded.

Habitués at Mrs. Smith's "at homes" and functions were sufficiently well acquainted with the lay of the house to tuck themselves into odd corners and alcoves; but both Talham and his apprehensive companion found themselves a little cramped for room in the tiny hall where six men were endeavouring to find pegs for their coats at one and the same time.

The drawing-room was on the first floor, and although the stairs leading up to it were somewhat narrow, Mrs. Smith carried out the illusion of a Foreign Office reception by receiving her guests on the first landing with her back to the bathroom door, and handing them over, as they squeezed past, to an ill-fitted butler, who conducted them the three or four paces which separated the end of stairs from the beginning of drawing-room.

She boasted that she never forgot names, and was wont to cite herself and King Edward as twin souls in this respect.

Indeed, from time to time, she found many startling phases of resemblance between herself and various members of the Royal Family.

The tiny drawing-room was uncomfortably crowded.

Tillizinni found himself wondering, as he pushed his way through the press, by what extraordinary manœuvre Mrs. Smith held and attracted such a large and representative body of good-looking young men.

He had a lurking suspicion that as fast as they entered the drawing-room by the door they surreptitiously escaped through the window.

There was that air of unreality which is frequently to be found in the small drawing-rooms of the people bitten by the social bug.

"She called me Mr. Tinker," said Talham's voice in the other's ear.

His words almost trembled with chagrin. Tillizinni tried to appease him.

"She called me Phillips," he said with a smile; "though that is not my name as far as I know. You must allow for lapses in the memory of a hostess who probably entertains thousands of people in a year."

Talham was silent, but he was very annoyed indeed.

The press was thickest at one end of the drawing-room, and to this the two made, following the instinct which invariably draws man to man—for men like men in crowds.

"What is the attraction?" grumbled Talham. "Is it not lamentable," he went on without waiting for a reply, which, as a matter of fact, the detective was not prepared to offer, "that with all the joyous and bountiful gifts which nature has prepared and laid open for her children, men should be found who prefer the hot and fetid atmosphere of a drawing-room and the stimulations of artificial gaiety to that ante-chamber of heaven, the field? Does not the pettiness—the inconclusiveness—of it, strike you? Think of the futility of effort——"

He got so far and was warming to his subject, when the little crowd which stood between them and the attraction, thinned, as a sea-fret thins before a westerly wind, and Tillizinni saw, for the first time in his life, Yvonne Yale.

She was standing near the fireplace, listening to a short youth by her side, with some evidence of boredom.

Her hair, perfectly coiffeured, was a mass of golden brown. About this she wore a little bandeau of dull gold.

Tillizinni received the impression of observing a crowned queen—so proud and straight she stood, with a little tilt to her chin, and the merest hint of condescension in her eyes, as she talked to the voluble youth who hung upon her words.

Her gown, cut low at the neck, was very plain. It was of black velvet, close fitting. About her neck she had three strings of imitation pearls. Her arms, bare to the elbow, were white and beautifully shaped; her hands larger than one expected, but pretty. She had a plain gold bangle about her wrist— the only jewel she wore.

Tillizinni looked at Talham. He was staring at the girl, his lips parted, his eyes wide open, his head a little forward.

At any other moment he would have amused the other, but Tillizinni had seen that look before—that strange earnestness and intensity with which he confronted the problems of life.

He continued to look, and the girl must have subconsciously become aware of the unwinking gaze fixed upon her, for she turned her head and faced him.

For a moment they stood thus, looking one at the other; then Tillizinni saw a delicate pink creep into her face, and he caught Talham's arm.

"Introduce me," he muttered, "and apologise for my rudeness."

Obeying rather the dictation of his inner self than any suggestion of his friend, Talham went towards her, his hand outstretched.

She held out her hand frankly with a little smile to Talham, and he took it. He held it, it seemed to Tillizinni, an unconscionable time. The responsibility of piloting Talham through the social maze was getting on the nerves of one who was famous throughout Europe for his freedom from nerve trouble.

"I am glad to see you again, Captain Talham," she said with a dazzling smile which showed two rows of pearly teeth. "We do not often entertain such distinguished people."

She said this with a gentle note of mockery, but as usual Talham took her very seriously.

"Whatever views you may hold regarding my friend," he said gravely, "you must not think of regarding me as distinguished. I hope, Miss Yale, that you and I shall be great friends. I will have no artificial barriers erected which may separate to any extent two people anxious to grow in acquaintance."

The girl looked puzzled. She had uttered the first conventional pleasantry which had come into her head. She never regarded Talham as distinguished.

To her he was a man, who in the moment of her necessity, had rendered a kindly and a chivalrous service.

She turned hurriedly, it seemed to Tillizinni, to introduce her mother—a lady dressed in the abrupt fashion which was suggestive of conflicting bargain sales.

Mrs. Smith was engaged in the eternal quest for the missing segment. It was only a tiny segment that was required to make both ends of her circle meet. She speculated modestly on the Stock Exchange, and dreamt dreams of meeting a magnificent, kindly man who would give her the "tip" of her life.

Then she would buy shares. The market would undergo some extraordinary evolution, and the shares she bought at one pound, less fortunate people would want to buy at twenty-five shillings. Then she would sell, and she would be exactly five shillings per share to the good.

And if she had had five thousand shares, why then she would have one thousand two hundred and fifty pounds.

It was very simple.

On such day dreams as these, men grow rich, but they are usually the men who sell the shares to the dreamers.

But Talham was not to be detached. He made a little speech to the mother, and with deplorable *sang froid*, dismissed her from the circle. It was unpardonable, but it was very much Talham.

Tillizinni, watching the scene with his keen eyes, was chuckling and learning.

But the girl was undoubtedly puzzled. She could not understand whether Talham was serious, or whether his persistence was a form of humour which had just about then become popular owing to the success of a certain socialist dramatist, with whose name I will not sully these fair pages.

"I am sure I shall be delighted," she murmured pleasantly.

He had invited her to a concert, and had in his magnetic, plausible way, persuaded her to go.

She altered her position, tapping her foot nervously—an infallible sign that she was embarrassed. She looked from Talham to the dark young man at her side.

Gregory de Costa owed his readmission to the Yale ménage to the admiration which Mrs. Smith had for his business acumen. There were some subjects which Yvonne did not regard as being worth a quarrel, and Gregory de Costa's attendance was one of these.

He made up for homeliness of face in magnificence of attire. His dress suit was cut so well that he seemed, like another famous character, to have been melted and poured into it. In the breast of his shirt blazed a diamond, almost as big as a hickory nut. His links, when he raised his hand to caress his tiny moustache, radiated light. His bejewelled fingers reminded one irresist-ibly of the illuminations at Luna Park.

"Do you know Mr. de Costa?" asked the girl.

Talham bowed to the young man, and the young man bowed to him.

For some reason she did not introduce Tillizinni.

"I think I have met you before, Captain Talham," said the young man.

"I do not think we have ever met you," said Talham with deliberation.

"In our office?" suggested Mr. de Costa, an encouraging smile on his thick lips.

"We have never been into your office," said Talham.

"I'm perfectly sure that I have seen you there," persisted the other.

If he expected that Talham would be satisfied with an exchange of plati-tudinous pleasantries with the girl, and then withdraw, he was disappointed. If he imagined he could draw Talham to a discussion on so futile a question as his presence in an office at some remote period of his life, he was mad.

Talham had a weightier interest. The thought that he might be *de trop* never occurred to him, and if it had been suggested that his unconventional method of interesting others in his career and his aspirations was calculated rather to bore than to grip their imaginations, he would have smiled, pity-ingly.

He diagnosed the girl's half-amused embarrassment as a natural ner-vousness in being suddenly confronted with a man of his attainments. By some extraordinary mental convolution which was peculiarly Talhamesque, he credited her with a full appreciation of his genius, a lurking suspicion of his identity, and a comfortable ignorance of the character of his adventures. Like the exigent little boy who demanded of the store-keeper two cents worth of hundreds and thousands—an infinitesimal candy, about the size of a pin's head, variously coloured—Talham wanted her to pick him out all white.

"It is more than a pleasure to again meet you, Miss Yale," he began, in his oratorical manner. "There are some events in life—some landmarks which rise above the dreary path that meanders across the plain of eternity—which stand out..."

He orated on without drawing breath, so to speak. For his imagery he ransacked forest and field and plain; the vegetable, mineral and animal king-doms contributed to the illuminations of his argument; and the girl stood look-ing at him wonderingly, a little frightened, a little—a very little—amused, a little—more than a little—bored.

As for Gregory de Costa—he stood stolidly by, taking no part in the conversation, twirling his moustache with a determined and an injured air.

From sheer humanity, Tillizinni set himself the task of diverting Tal-ham's attention. He felt that his action was invested with that heroism which one reads about in books of travel, when a devoted servant sets himself the thankless task of attracting the attention of a tiger, feeding upon his fellow creature, to his plump and trembling self.

Tillizinni succeeded, however, in giving the girl an opportunity for escape; but he drew down upon himself all the heavy weapons in Talham's arsenal. It was absolutely necessary for him to seek out Mrs. Smith and pay her that little attention which is due from a guest to his hostess.

Fortunately Mrs. Smith came to the rescue. She was engaged in that process which is described in the society columns as "mixing up her guests." In other words, she was making her slow way through the crowded little room, giving a nod here, a smile there, some comment—generally misplaced—elsewhere. She left behind her a trail of bachelors, who had, in acknowledging her tender inquiries after their wives, inferentially admitted such possessions.

She found Talham, and from the manner in which she pounced upon him and led him forth, Tillizinni gathered that the object of her search had been accomplished.

She was Yvonne Yale's stepmother, being the second wife of the gallant colonel who had long since passed over to the majority. Mrs. Smith's poetical way of putting it, was that he had taken his sword to heaven; but as to this, it is impossible to speak with authority.

She was one of those women who have a den—half study, half boudoir, all roll-top desks and Liberty knick-knacks. She prided herself upon being a thorough business woman, with a head for figures, which meant periodical disputes between her and her broker, which induced piles of tragic correspondence between herself and her bank, and explained to a very large extent the domestic cataclysms which were of such frequent occurrence in her household.

To this den she led Talham, and in the hour he spent with her he learnt as much of her private history, and much more of her financial standing, than she knew herself.

He came back and rescued Tillizinni at a period where he was bored to the point of tears. Talham was very important and very mysterious. He plunged into the crowd again to find Yvonne Yale. She may have seen him coming; at any rate Tillizinni saw her look helplessly round, then face him with a scared look.

"Must you really go, Captain Talham?"

Talham said that he really must go; he said why he had to go, what he had to do—the hours of anxious work which lay ahead of him—and he hinted of the destinies of people which would be affected by any longer abstention from their interest. He spoke of generations yet unborn whose fates were trembling in the balance; he laid down the well-worn thesis that social obligations should be subservient to stern economic realities.

If she thought she had seen the last of him after he had so unmistakably expressed his intention of retiring, she was mistaken. She did not know Talham. She felt foolish and resented the cause. People at whom speeches are made in public invariably feel foolish.

Yet for all the exhaustive character of his farewell, Talham remembered on his way home several things he had intended to say, and was half inclined to go back to say them. All the way to the hotel he could think of nothing else but her wonderful eyes, her refinement, her glorious voice.

She was, he then told me, the daughter of an army officer who had died suddenly a few years before, leaving the second wife and his daughter the most meagre of incomes. This was the text on which he delivered an address, dealing with the duty of the state and the grudging gratitude of the nation. So far as Tillizinni was able to trace, Yvonne's father was a colonel of infantry, who had spent some twenty years in various parts of the globe, missing active service the whole of his life, and finishing up with the command of a militia depôt. Under these circumstances, Talham's heroics about the "children of England's battle-scarred defenders" were beside the point.

"Mrs. Yale," he said impressively, "was a wonderful woman, a splendid woman, a business woman. I can only hope that Yvonne inherits her splendid qualities."

When Talham ordered his world to his own satisfaction, he was not above adjusting the laws of progeniture. Mrs. Smith had sought his advice as to her investments. Talham had fallen for it.

It is a subtle form of flattery employed by dowagers, who could not hint at the physical attractions of their middle-aged and bald-headed admirers, and still retain their self-respect; and who found in this oblique tribute to their business capacities an effective and profitable substitute.

But Talham was not middle-aged, and the poison of the flattery had eaten deeper into his system.

"I am transferring five thousand shares in the Mount Li Exploration Syndicate," he said.

Tillizinni was not easily moved, but now he gasped.

"The Mount Li——?" he asked incredulously.

"The Mount Li Exploration Syndicate," said Talham firmly.

"But there isn't such a company," protested the other.

Talham looked at him a little sadly.

"It is one of the things I have overlooked," he said. "One of the essentials of our communal life. It did not, I confess, occur to me until that extraordinary woman was discussing such things as shares and bonds, that I realised in a flash that it was impossible for me to help her because no such shares stood in my name. Have not," he asked impressively, "the great events of history which have transformed the world, been born in a moment's inspiration? Even as I sat there, in the excellently appointed study—I must make a note, by the way, of the furnishing of that apartment: I should like an office arranged on similar lines—the Mount Li Exploration came into existence."

"In other words," said Tillizinni with a helpless smile, "you created the company in order to give her shares!"

"I created the company," agreed the tall man, gravely.

CHAPTER 8

THE CELESTIAL WAY

IT was a drizzling, miserable night; the streets were crowded with cars and cabs carrying their occupants to theatreland. On the drenched pavements the newspaper boys drove a thriving trade despite the unpromising climatic conditions. Every news bill dealt with the one subject—the mysterious murder, in the heart of London, of an ambassador by some person or persons unknown.

That it was the Chinese Ambassador added to the general interest. There was something bizarre and mysterious about the great empire which appealed to the imagination, and the series of hypothesis which appeared in the columns of the press assisted to a remarkable degree in fostering the sense of mystery which surrounded the tragedy.

There was scarcely a police-station in London that was not at that moment interrogating some stray Chinaman who had been brought in to account for his whereabouts on the night of the murder.

There was not a district, apparently, which could not furnish a clue.

The Evening Megaphone, London's most enterprising evening journal, secured something of a "beat," for it was the only paper which was able to throw a light upon the inside mystery of a vendetta which had apparently culminated in the Ambassador's assassination.

"We are able," said this journal, in large, leaded type, "to supply a number of curious and significant facts concerning the tragedy, which have hitherto been unrecorded elsewhere. Our representative had the pleasure of a long conversation with Mr. T'si Soo, a wealthy young Chinese gentleman who has been domiciled in England for a number of years. Mr. T'si Soo is the son of the Governor of Chulung, a large and populous district of China, and is engaged in this city in studying constitutional law. Mr. Soo—a fine, handsome-looking young man of commanding appearance—received the representative of *The Evening Megaphone* in Piccadilly. Fortunately Mr. Soo has a perfect command of English, and the interpreter which our representative brought with him was unnecessary.

"'I cannot tell you,' said Mr. Soo, 'how grieved I am at the death of the Noble Prince who so ably and worthily represented the Dowager Empress at the court of St. James.

"'The Prince, as you know, was an antiquarian of great note, but he was also a man of strong political opinions which, I fear, have not always commended themselves to the majority of my fellow countrymen.

"'He was by repute a reactionary,' he went on, 'and earned the animosity of a number of secret societies in China by his efforts to secure their abolition.'

"'But surely,' our representative pointed out, 'the abolition of secret societies is not a reactionary movement!'

"Mr. Soo shook his head.

"'You are now speaking,' he said with a smile, 'from the point of view of the European. In China we regard anybody as a reactionary who attempts to alter the position of affairs so that it corresponds with any period of time in the past. For instance, there was a time when there were no secret societies; to abolish them would be regarded, therefore, as a reactionary measure since it would produce conditions which had once existed. That, again, I say, is an Eastern point of view.'

"'Do you explain the murder as having been committed by the emissary of a society?' asked our representative.

"Mr. Soo nodded.

"'I believe there is an association,' he said, 'which had a special reason for removing the Ambassador.'

"'It has been suggested,' said our representative, 'that robbery was the object of the murder, and that a bureau had been rifled and valuable documents extracted.'

"Mr. Soo was very emphatic in dissociating himself with this theory.

"'That I do not believe,' he said. 'The people who killed his Excellency probably travelled all the way from China, and are now, possibly, on their way back again. They had no other object but his destruction, and if they stole documents, they were documents associated with the Prince's campaign to suppress the societies affected.'

"It may be remarked," continued the enterprising journal, "that such is the abhorrence in which the crime is held by every Chinaman, that numerous offers of help have come to this paper from Chinese citizens who desire to assist in the search for the miscreant. It may be said that the interpreter who accompanied our representative was one of these. It was through his instrumentality that the interview with Mr. Soo was secured.

"With extraordinary modesty, he disappeared as soon as the interview was concluded, and has since not been in this office."

Whilst the contents bills of *The Evening Megaphone* were flaring the question at every street corner: "Was Ambassador Killed by Secret Society?" Soo himself was interviewing the interpreter whose enterprise and modesty the journal was at the moment praising. He was interviewing him in a little room, the smallest in the suite he occupied, and he was assisted in the process by three compatriots, who gazed impassively on a Chinaman, a little less impassive, stretched upon a small iron bed, his wrists strapped to the bed head, his feet spreadeagled and strapped to its sides.

Soo sat on a chair smoking his inevitable cigarette, with his inevitable monocle glued in his eye, watching the man with interest.

"First," he said, "you shall tell me why you came here, who sent you, and what you desired."

"Lord," gasped the man on the bed, "I have told you everything; by my Father's grace I have nothing more to say."

His face was drawn and haggard, beads of perspiration stood upon his shaven skull, and terror was in his eyes.

"You shall tell me," repeated the other calmly, "who sent you, why you came, and what you were told to do."

He nodded to the man who sat nonchalantly smoking a pipe by the side of the captive's bed.

The man leant over and made a half turn of the screw upon a weird-shaped contrivance which enclosed the prisoner's fingers.

The man suppressed a shriek with reason, for over him leant a second Chinaman ready to thrust a gag in his mouth.

"You shall tell me," said Soo monotonously, "why you came, who sent you here, and your business."

"Lord," whispered the man, "I will tell you all I know."

Soo nodded to the torturer, and he loosened the screw on the other's finger.

"Give him water," said Soo, and the attendant with the gag put a cup to the other's lips. He drank greedily.

"Lord, I was sent by my society, which, as your Excellency knows, is the society of the 'Banner Bearers of Heaven.'"

Soo nodded.

"They desired to discover how your Lordship felt in this matter."

"To whom were you to report?" asked Soo.

The man hesitated, and his interrogator glanced significantly at the screw in which the captive's hand still rested. It was enough for the man on the bed.

He mentioned a name.

Soo recognised it as the keeper of a Chinese lodging-house in the East End of London—a man who was known to him to be the agent of the Bannermen.

CHAPTER 9

THE ABDUCTION

YVONNE YALE had spent a tiring and a busy day shopping with her mother. It was not a relaxation which she often allowed herself. Mrs. Yale took shopping very seriously, and would follow a will-o'-the-wisp of a five-shilling bargain through enticing marshes of other departments where scarcely a weed grew which was not labelled twenty-five shillings.

After dinner, Mrs. Yale announced the fact that she was dead tired; she implied the further fact that the exertions of the day, shared by her daughter, had not effected her, and that the energy dissipated by Mrs. Yale herself was sufficient for two.

She went to bed, leaving Yvonne half a dozen letters to answer—letters which regretted the inability of Mrs. Yale to settle an account, but promised "next month," not only to clear off existing liabilities, but to extend her scope of patronage.

Yvonne's self-respect led her to tone down the letters, to make them less optimistic as to the future and less vague as to the present. She finished her work at half-past eleven, and signed her mother's name with a flourish, enclosed the letters in envelopes, and placed them on the hall table ready for posting.

She made her customary round of the house—their one servant was in bed at that hour—and went to her room feeling depressed and worried. She could not trace her state of mind to any particular course, and she told herself that the reason was purely physical. She undressed in record time, jumped into bed, switched out the light, and her head had hardly touched the pillow before she was asleep.

How long she had been sleeping she could not tell, but something woke her with a start. The room was dark, the only light being that from the lamp in the street below. She was wide awake, and her reasoning faculty told her that something must have occurred—there must have been some extraordinary noise to have brought about this condition of wakefulness.

She lay perfectly still—listening. For a long time she heard nothing and saw nothing; then for a moment she saw a tiny streak of bright light in the room.

Before she could touch it her wrist was grasped, and a long, bony hand closed over her mouth.

"Be silent!" said a voice in her ear. "If you make a noise I will kill you!"

She felt a grip on her throat, and lay paralysed with terror; she had neither the will nor the ability to scream.

At last she found her voice.

"Take what you want and go," she said.

"Where do you keep your jewels?" said the man who held her, in a low voice.

The ghost of a smile, in spite of the tragic situation, dawned on Yvonne's face.

"In the top drawer of my bureau," she said, and might have added: "such as they are"; but even her sense of humour could not rise equal to the occasion.

The man muttered some words in a language which she could not understand; but she gathered that he was addressing the second man in the room, for two there were undoubtedly.

Then with a sickening sense of danger she realised that the language was Chinese.

She heard the soft "hush" of the drawer as it opened, she saw the flash of light as the men swept it over her belongings. Then the man at the drawer spoke over his shoulder. There was a quick exchange of words, then:

"Get up!" said the man by her side shortly.

There was nothing to do but obey. She rose from her bed and stood on the floor shaking in every limb. She was thankful for the darkness which perhaps hid the full extent of her danger.

"You have a bracelet somewhere," said the man who had spoken first. "It was given to you by young De Costa. Where is it now?"

The girl made no reply. She was dismayed when she realised that Talham's deception had been discovered, and she felt herself a guilty party to the deception.

"I have not got it," she said.

"Who has?" The voice was sharp and authoritative.

"Captain Talham has it," she said, before she realised that she was betraying the strange man. He was nothing to her, yet even in the moment of her peril, she understood that perhaps she might be endangering him, and was sorry she had spoken.

There was a little silence, then:

"Put on your clothes!" said the man.

"Why?" she asked startled.

"Don't argue. You can dress in the dark. Put on your clothes. If you can't I'll turn on the light."

She groped for her clothes, thankful to dress in the dark, and the man walked over to the door.

"Remember," he said as his vice-like grip released her arm, "any attempt to raise an alarm will result in your immediate death; there are no men in this house as I know. Captain Talham, on whom you may unreasonably depend, is quite unconscious of your present predicament. I am going to take you away from here, and I swear to you that you shall not be harmed. Are you going to take my word?"

"There is no alternative," answered the girl.

With trembling hands she drew on her clothes. That she should be dressing herself in the presence of two Chinamen—for a Chinaman the first speaker was, in spite of his perfect English—did not strike her at the moment as being so much a subject for dismay, as to what would happen after she had dressed.

There was a heavy cloak hanging in the wardrobe of the room. She drew this on over her other things, and, twisting her hair into a knot at the top of her head, fixed a hat over what she knew was a most appalling untidiness.

"It may not be necessary," said the man, "to tell you that any cry will bring your mother and the maid—in which case I shall destroy not only you, but the people you alarm."

He guided her past her mother's door, down the stairs and into the street.

A little distance from the door was a motor-car. The second man went out, and at a signal the car drew across the road to the door of the house.

She was hustled inside, and the two men sprang in after her. With a jerk the car started upon the most adventurous journey that Yvonne Yale had ever taken in her short, and until then, uneventful, career.

Just as the car passed out of sight, a taxi came flying round the corner, and pulled up at the door of Mrs. Yale's dwelling. Two men got out and made straight for the door. The first of these was Tillizinni. He had his hand upon the knocker when he felt the door yield to his touch, and he pushed it open.

He turned to the pale-faced Talham.

"My God!" he said. "They've been here!"

He slipped a revolver from his hip pocket, and went up the stairs, two at a time, for Talham had found the switch which controlled the stair light.

Tillizinni guessed that the best bedroom would be at the back, and that Mrs. Yale would occupy it.

He knocked on the door.

"Who's there?" asked a muffled voice.

"Open, please!" said Tillizinni. "I am an officer of police, and I want to see you very urgently."

Mrs. Yale came out to the light of the detective's lamp and presented an unhappy figure.

"Which room does your daughter occupy?" asked Tillizinni.

She recognised Talham with an embarrassed smile.

"My daughter is in the next room." She led the way and knocked at the door; but again there was no necessity for knocking—the door was half open. She entered, followed without invitation by Tillizinni, who was too anxious as to the girl's safety to stand upon ceremony.

The bed was empty. He put his hand inside—it was still warm. A quick glance round at the open drawers gave evidence of the visitors' presence.

There was no time to be lost.

"Your daughter has been kidnapped," he said. "You must arouse your servants. I will send a policeman to you."

Into the street again came the two men, and Tillizinni lifted one of the lamps from the taxi and examined the roadway. There had been a sharp shower of rain half an hour previous, and the tracks of the other car were plainly visible.

He ran along the roadway carrying the lamp, and reached the thoroughfare which ran to the north and south. There was no evidence that the car had taken either direction. He crossed the road, the taxi-cab following in his rear. Yes, here it was again—the broad band had gone straight on. They would be making now for Portland Place.

At this point a policeman appeared, and Tillizinni gave him an order that set the man running back to the house in Curzon Street. Then Tillizinni went back to the cab, and the taxi went straight ahead at full speed, slowing at the point where Portland Place cut across the route.

The streets were newly washed. Indeed, the great thoroughfare was at that moment in the hands of the scavengers with their hoses and their squeegees. There would be no definite track here, and Tillizinni, after a search, saw sufficient evidence to show him which direction the car had taken.

At Oxford Circus a policeman had seen it. It had turned eastward, and had gone straight along Oxford Street in the direction of Holborn.

"Speed up!" said Tillizinni to the driver. "There's just a chance they may have a puncture, and we may overtake them."

He rejoined the silent Talham in the cab.

"I'll never forgive myself," said the big man. He sat with his hands clasped together, and his face set.

"My dear chap, it's not your fault."

Tillizinni laid his hand on the other's shoulder. He had a genuine affection for this eccentric giant with his irrepressible oratory and his calm disregard for convention.

"It's a damned bracelet," said Talham bitterly. "All the wealth and all the secrets of Ts'in are too inadequate compensation for one moment of misery she may suffer."

Tillizinni made no reply. Like a white light it suddenly dawned upon him that this man, the last man in the world that he would have imagined, was smitten with love.

The tense agony in Talham's voice, the attitude of absolute dejection—he sat huddled in a corner of the cab—spoke eloquently of his agony.

At Holborn Bars a City policeman had seen a car passing swiftly eastward, and yet again, and farther on at the Mansion House, a patrolling sergeant was able to direct them toward Gracechurch Street.

They lost the scent at Tower Hill. Two cars had come along at about the same moment, probably one from Eastcheap. One had crossed Tower Bridge and gone southward; the other had continued its way eastward. Unfortunately both had been of similar make.

Tillizinni was in a dilemma.

"We'll take the east road," he said, after a moment's thought; "that is the more likely route."

A moment later the cab was following the trail of an empty car on its way to Harwich to meet the morning boat.

CHAPTER 10

THE ROOMS BY THE CANAL

YVONNE YALE had sat in silence during that mad rush through the City. Once in a frenzy of terror she had half risen to throw herself from the car. Instantly Soo's hand grasped her.

"When I tell you I will kill you, I mean it," he said quickly. "Be quiet, and no harm will come to you. I tell you this, that I am merely holding you as a hostage for the recovery of the bangle. If I know your friend, he will not hesitate when he knows a woman is in danger."

His words reassured her somewhat. She had hardly dared to put her fears into words.

The car swung round Tower Hill and slowed at the very spot where Tillizinni was destined to stop ten minutes later; but it did not go eastward, as Tillizinni had thought, but crossed the bridge, sped down the slope into Tooley Street, turned again, and followed the Deptford Road.

It continued until it came to a street which ran parallel with the north bank of the Surrey Canal, and into this it turned. It was a street made up of wharf entrances, of old and dilapidated warehouses and stables.

The car stopped before a low-roofed old building that in its prosperous days had been part of the wharfage of a stone merchant. As the car stopped, a door in the wall opened, and Soo flung away the cigarette which he had smoked during the latter part of the journey, stepped quickly to the ground, and half dragged and half carried the fainting girl into the building. Instantly the car moved on, and the door closed behind her.

They were in complete darkness. There was a musty, unwholesome smell. The atmosphere of the place filled her with cold terror.

"This way!" said Soo.

He led her unerringly across the ramshackle shed. At the far end there was a door which opened and revealed a room lit by two swinging oil lamps.

It was poorly furnished, with a table and a couple of chairs, and a fire blazed in a broken grate in one corner. Some attempt had been made to produce a sense of comfort—the square of carpet on the floor, and the plain table-cover had evidently been newly purchased and still showed their shop creases.

The room was untenanted, and Soo and the girl entered alone. He closed the door behind him.

She saw now a man in the garb of a Westerner, whose face was hidden from her by a curious contrivance. This was no less than a waxen mask, which fitted the upper portion of the face down to the mouth. So skilfully and cunningly had the colours been blended, that it was difficult to see where the real ended and the artificial began. It gave the man a European appearance, and made him tolerably good-looking.

He locked the door, then turned and faced her.

"You stay here, Miss Yale," he said, "until I secure satisfaction from your friend. This," he explained, waving his hand round the apartment, "was once the manager's quarters. It is fitted with some luxury."

He opened a little door.

"There is a bathroom here," he said, "and you will find everything you may desire."

"How long do you intend to keep me?" she asked.

It was the first coherent question she had put to him.

He shrugged his shoulders.

"That depends entirely upon the willingness of your friend to give me what I wish," he answered.

"You know you are committing a very grave crime," she said, "and that you will be punished for this?"

She saw a smile gather on the thin lips.

"I have a much more extensive knowledge of the criminal law of England than you can be expected to have," he said coolly. "I am well aware of all the risks I take; but since I am prepared to take the additional, and to you, perhaps, unthinkable, risk of losing my life, the minor perils need not be counted."

Without another word he left her. She waited until the sound of his footsteps had died away; then she made a quick examination of the two rooms.

From the sitting-room a door opened into a tiny bedroom. It was scrupulously clean; the sheets were of the finest linen, pillow of down, and what other furniture occupied the room was in good taste.

There was one small window, heavily barred, and screened from the street by an opaque pane of toughened glass. She was to learn that this looked upon a small wharf, and that no help might be expected from that direction. There was a little window in the bathroom which also looked out upon another corner of the wharf.

The sitting-room depended entirely upon artificial light. So she thought until she looked up and saw a big skylight in the room.

She returned to the little bedroom and found, with considerable satisfaction, that a much needed brush and comb had been provided. She dressed her hair and washed her face in the little bathroom.

There was no question of sleeping that night. It encouraged her, and removed some of her apprehension to find how thoroughly her abductor had prepared for her arrival. There was a bookshelf, well stocked with the latest novels, and if the selection had been a hasty one, it was also a wise one.

She came back to the fire and drew up a chair, for she felt cold. "What would be the end?" She shivered, and dare not supply an answer. She got up and walked to the door and listened. There was no sound outside. It came on to rain, and the pitter-patter of the drops as they fell upon the tiled roof gave her a sense of companionship with the outside world.

She wondered when her mother would discover her absence. She was unlikely to make her discovery before nine o'clock in the morning.

What would she do? Would she call in the police? Would that extraordinary man, Tillizinni, endeavour to fathom the mystery of her disappearance? She prayed that he would. And Talham?

She found herself thinking more of Talham than she could have thought possible. He liked her—she was sure of it. She was afraid that the impecunious Captain of Irregular Horse was in love with her.

She shook her head a little impatiently at the thought. Why could not the friendship exist about which the philosopher wrote? Why could not a woman possess a man friend without the disagreeable element coming into it?

Talham was responsible for her present plight; yet she did not blame him, which was a curious circumstance for a woman untouched by love. She was satisfied at least that of all the people who would be affected by the news of her disappearance, he would feel his responsibility most poignantly.

She walked up and down the little room. It must have been half an hour after Soo departed that he came back again.

He opened the door quietly and stepped inside, locking it again after him, and laid on the table a letter. It was typed, she noticed, and was addressed to Captain Talham.

"You will sign this," said Soo briefly. He read it over. It was short and to the point. It ran:

"Dear Captain Talham,—I am at present in the hands of some people who desire you to restore the jade bracelet, which, as you know, you took from me.

"Unless you do this within forty-eight hours either I shall be killed or worse will happen to me. I implore you, therefore, to hand the bracelet to a messenger who will meet you to-night at six o'clock in Whitcombe Court, Coventry Street."

She read the letter through, and looked up at the man.

"What guarantee have I," she asked, "if I sign this letter, and if Captain Talham is in a position to restore the bracelet, that you will keep your part of the bargain, and will release me?"

"You have no guarantee at all," he said coolly, "except my word. But I am in this position, that you must accept my word without any proof of my bona-fides."

She hesitated before she took the fountain-pen which he offered her. She read the letter through again.

There was no harm in signing it. She would be no better off by refusing, and she might easily be worse. She was cool-headed now.

She signed her name at the foot of the sheet, and handed it to him.

He took it from her with a little bow.

"Perhaps you would like to write some letters," he said. "You will find paper in the drawer of the table, and if by any chance you have any correspondence you would like to clear off in this uncomfortable period of waiting, this will be an excellent opportunity."

His tone was polite, he was not even mildly sarcastic. He wished to convey to her the fact that her detention was a temporary business, a regrettable expedient which need occasion her no alarm.

"Suppose Captain Talham refuses to give this up," she said, "as he may very well do; or suppose he has parted with it and is not in a position to hand it to you, what happens to me?"

She asked the question calmly, and the man shrugged his shoulders.

"I will accept no excuses," he said. "Whatever happens, subsequent to his refusal, will be most regrettable." With which sinister remark he left her.

She stood near the door. She thought she heard voices outside. Quick voices speaking in low tones excitedly, and she wondered who was the masked man's companion.

She was soon to learn, for the door opened, and Soo came in, followed by four Chinamen.

"Get your coat on!" he said roughly. "We have got to get out of here at once."

"What is the matter?" she asked.

"Get your coat on!" he said, ignoring her question. "I haven't a moment to spare."

All his polish had dropped away.

She had known him for a Chinaman despite his mask, and she knew there was nothing to be gained by opposing one of the race which places women on the level of domestic animals. She went into the bedroom and put on her cloak, again pinned on her hat, and came out to where the men were waiting.

They were talking eagerly together in Chinese.

"I am going to take you for a little journey by water," said Soo.

He extinguished the light in the room, and led the way noiselessly across the empty warehouse to a big door which led out on to the wharf. It was a sliding door, which moved noiselessly upon its greased guides.

Soo stepped out first, and the girl followed. Ahead of her she saw a patch of untidy wharf and the dull gleam of water. He piloted her to the edge of the wharf and peered down into the canal; but there was no sign of a boat.

He turned and hissed a savage enquiry to one of his companions.

The girl's heart beat high, instinct told her that help was on the way, and the absence of the boat was at least a respite.

"Quick!" said Soo. "Come!"

He caught her by the arm, and she half ran and half walked back to the building, through the barn-like warehouse, and to the door through which they had first entered.

"Remember," he said, "that any sound you make will bring upon you consequences which you will have very little time for regretting."

He pulled back the bolt, and the door swung open noiselessly. He had his hand upon the girl's arm, and his foot was raised to step across the threshold when a flood of white light struck him, and he staggered back.

"Put up your hands!" said a voice.

It was the voice of Tillizinni.

CHAPTER 11

CAPTAIN TALHAM'S PROGRESS

FOR a second only Soo stood. He saw the gleam of two pistol barrels directed at his breast, and then with a sudden jerk of his arm, he brought the girl into the line of fire.

A second later, he was running with all speed across the building and through the gate.

He heard fleet footsteps coming after him, and looking over his shoulder he saw the tall form of Talham silhouetted in the doorway of the warehouse. He could have shot him then, and was tempted to take the risk, but thought better of it. A shot would arouse the neighbourhood, would set whistles blowing, and might perhaps dissipate his last chance of escape.

He could trust his men to preserve his secret. He sped without hesitation to the end of the wharf. The boat was still away. He understood now why it had not put in an appearance. He heard a whistle blow, and cursed himself for his failure to make use of an opportunity of killing Talham which the gods had put into his hands.

The place was surrounded—he guessed that. He guessed it just as soon as he understood the significance of the boat's absence. There was no time to hesitate, without a pause he leapt from the edge of the wharf into the dark and noisome waters of the canal. He came to the surface for a moment to breathe, and cast his eyes back to the bank.

Innumerable beams of light were searching the water. The police had recently been equipped with a new truncheon torch.

He could swim under water like a fish, and he did not come up again until the black hulk of a moored barge offered protection from the prying eyes of the police.

"He's gone, I'm afraid!" said Tillizinni with an expression of vexation. "I'd like to have seen his face."

"But didn't you see it?" asked Talham in astonishment.

"I saw an ingenious mask," said the other.

"I thought it was curious," said Talham, "that a European could run as that man ran. He had that curious sideways waddle which only the Chinks have."

They were talking in the little warehouse, half filled with police now, and bright with light. Four Chinamen sat on the ground handcuffed together and philosophical.

"I could have wished to capture the car," said Tillizinni. "I might then have found its owner. Yet"—he turned a dazzling smile upon the girl—"we have succeeded in doing what we set out to accomplish."

She looked very white and shaky, and Talham was no less pale.

"I am grateful this has turned out so well for me," she said softly.

Tillizinni explained how they had taken the wrong road, and how by great good fortune they had come upon the car they were chasing drawn up at a coffee stall, where the chauffeur was taking an early morning breakfast. They had got back to Tower Bridge, and picked up the trail with no difficulty, save that none had seen the car turn into the little street which runs by the side of the canal. Here, however, the two men had to do some quick guessing, and once in the little *cul de sac*, the hiding place had easily been located.

Exactly how, he did not explain, but two hours later he was comparing the cigarette end which he had picked up outside of the warehouse with one Talham had found in Mr. de Costa's study.

"I don't know whether this is enough to issue a warrant on," he said. "It would be quite sufficient for the detective in fiction"—he smiled—"but unfortunately police magistrates have little imagination and no romance, and require something more substantial in the shape of evidence than the characteristics of Chinese tobacco."

* * * *

An ordinary man would have waited a day or two before he attempted to renew acquaintance with a woman whose charms had created so profound an impression upon him, and moreover, who had been responsible for so much mental suffering on the part of the woman whom he loved. But Talham was no ordinary man. He called the next day, and having no more idea of social conventions than a cow has of painting on silk, he chose a quarter to one in the afternoon as the hour.

Mercifully, both Mrs. Yale and her daughter were indulging in the luxury of a day's shopping, and Talham came back to Adelphi Terrace crestfallen, and sat moodily at the lunch table watching his host eat. Tillizinni expostulated with him.

"It was absurd to call at an hour like that," he said.

"I thought they might ask me to lunch," said Talham naïvely.

He refused to eat anything for a little while, and then his healthy appetite overcame his desire for starving to death, with the result that the detective had to wait another three-quarters of an hour at the table whilst he fed, which annoyed him intensely.

"Do you think if I called this afternoon——" he asked tentatively.

"You'll make yourself a nuisance. Moreover," Tillizinni said as a bright idea struck him, "Miss Yale will not unnaturally think that we regard our rescue of her as giving us the right of entrance into the house at all inconvenient hours of the day and night."

His face fell, and he made no attempt to put his threat of calling into execution. Indeed, during the next few days he was so busy with his preparation for departure, that Tillizinni hoped that his infatuation had died a natural death. When, later, he mentioned the material prospects of the Yales, Tillizinni was sufficiently indiscreet as to suggest that they might be well left to work out their own salvation.

"It is to such unsympathetic pharisaical souls as yours," he said, amongst other things, "that we owe the shocking and cynical disregard for infant life in England, the deterioration of the national physique, the growth of anti-militist in France."

On the fourth day after the abduction, Talham called. At four o'clock in the afternoon he issued from his room at the Pall Mall Palace Hotel arrayed like a modern Solomon in all his glory. From the tips of his enamelled American shoes, to the crown of his glossy Bond Street hat, he was the man about town.

In an hour and a half, considerably agitated, he called upon Tillizinni. Whatever had happened he did not say, but he directed the vials of his wrath upon two gentlemen who had had the singular bad taste to be present, and to monopolise much of the lady's time during Talham's visit.

Talham would have sent them out, but they had apparently called to take the girl out to a "five o'clock."

"It was impossible to say what I wanted to say," he said moodily, striding up and down the apartment, "so I hit upon a ruse."

He shrugged his shoulders.

"What was the ruse?" asked Tillizinni; but the other seemed disinclined to go on.

"In love as in war," he began at last, "all means are justified. Remembering the seriousness of the issue, remembering the tremendous effect which the decision one way or the other might produce upon posterity, and remembering, too, that in love as in war, as I say, we come against the elementary passions which are superior to the trivial conventions of modern life——"

Tillizinni waited, wonderingly.

"My suggestion to the two young men—one, as I have told you, was De Costa, and the other a Mr. William Dixon, of forty-three, Claremont Gardens, S.W.," he added imposingly and significantly, "my suggestion was, I contend, perfectly pardonable and quite admissible within the rules of war. It was that I had a friend who in a moment of exuberation had struck a police-man."

Tillizinni gasped.

"As a result of that unlawful act, my friend had been arrested and taken to Bow Street police station, the police being ignorant as to his identity. I myself was a stranger in the country; I had not sufficient influence to secure his release. Would these gentlemen of their charity drive to Bow Street and vouch for the respectability of my unfortunate friend?"

He said all this hesitatingly, yet hurriedly; there were long pauses between each sentence. Talham was obviously ill at ease.

"And who," Tillizinni asked slowly, "might this unfortunate friend of yours be?"

Talham looked at the ceiling thoughtfully.

"If by any chance," he said, "I have overstepped——"

"Not me!" cried the detective in horror. "You didn't say it was me?"

Talham nodded silently.

"I will only say this in extenuation," he said with that seriousness which made all his actions so real and plausible: "that I took particular care to impress upon them that you were perfectly sober."

Tillizinni fell back in the chair helplessly, with silent laughter.

"Well?" he asked at last. "Having resigned myself to the loss of what little character I possessed, I should like to know what these two young people did?"

"I must confess," said Talham, "that they were very decent. They went at once, took a taxi-cab, and drove straight away to the police station. Not finding you there, and ascertaining by telephone that you were not at Adelphi Terrace, they came back. In the meantime I had thrown myself upon the mercy of Yvonne."

"Did you call her Yvonne?" Tillizinni asked.

"I called her Yvonne," said Talham gravely, "because that is her name. I put before her as much of my prospects as I deemed it expedient to reveal. I gave her a brief resumé of my views of love and matrimony and the duty which we owe to the future. I told her in the terms which I have discovered are usual"—(It was afterwards discovered that Talham had sent out a comprehensive commission to the nearest bookstall for all the latest novels in which love dominated)—"that I loved her, and would endeavour by a life-long service, by a devotion which should be unique in the history of the world, to make her life an increasing joy and pleasure."

He was walking up and down all the time he spoke. He stopped in front of the window and stared out. Thunder clouds were banking up over South London, and on the murky horizon there was the flicker of lightning.

"That is as it should be," he said.

Talham was approving of the elements; it was not the first time he had suggested that the incidence of natural phenomena were directed by an all-wise Providence to coincide with his moods.

"She could not agree," he said. "She was startled, I thought at first that she was angry; but possibly I am doing her an injustice."

"What of the young men?"

"They returned as I was going," said Talham.

He swung round on Tillizinni.

"I have their cards and their addresses; that is what I wish to see you about. If you are my friend, you will call on them to-morrow and arrange a meeting."

The detective had no words; he simply arose from the chair with his mouth open.

"Arrange a meeting!" he stammered.

"Arrange a meeting," said Talham. "They used language to me which I will not permit any man to use. Moreover, what they said was in the presence of my future wife."

"But she refused you!"

"My future wife," repeated Talham in such a tone of decision as left no room for argument.

"But what do you mean by a meeting? You don't for one moment imagine that these people will fight a duel?"

"That remains to be seen," said the other. "I think that Hyde Park in the early hours of the morning would be an admirable rendezvous. You may leave to them the choice of weapons. I know very little about these fancy small swords which duellists favour, but if they will be kind enough to choose cavalry swords, I should be glad. I will fight them with Chinese knives, or, of course, with rapiers, if they prefer those weapons. I have no doubt that I shall make myself proficient in a few hours. As honourable men, they will not, of course, desire to take me at a disadvantage."

He discussed the punctilio of duelling at some length. There was no use in arguing with him.

They spent the evening together, Tillizinni examining the documents which had been removed from the Chinese Embassy, and Talham assisting him.

"You understand, of course," the detective explained, "that if I come upon any information which is likely to be of service to you in your search for your tomb——"

"Not my tomb," corrected Talham.

"Well, the Emperor's tomb," said the other. "I cannot allow you to see it."

"You will find nothing," said Talham with confidence. "Every scrap referring to the Tomb of the First Emperor was in the stolen docket."

It was nearly half-past ten when his servant brought Tillizinni a card. The detective read it and passed it to the other. It was inscribed:

RAYMOND DE COSTA
&
GREGORY DE COSTA.

The two exchanged glances.

"Show them up!" said Tillizinni.

Talham's face brightened up.

"I wonder——" he began, but did not finish his sentence. It might have been that he imagined that the visit would symbolise an act of self-abnegation of which young De Costa was incapable.

All his doubts were disposed of a few minutes later when the sulky young man, looking stouter and more unpleasant than ever, came into the room and introduced his father.

De Costa bowed ceremoniously to both men.

"This is my father," said young De Costa.

Something made Tillizinni look at Talham. He had the faintest of smiles upon his lips, as at some amusing recollection.

"You know my father, I think," said young De Costa.

"I haven't that pleasure," replied Talham.

The older man favoured him with a malicious little grin.

"I think we have done business together, Mr.—er—Talham."

"Is it Talham?" asked the other innocently. "I seem to remember another name. May I sit down?"

Tillizinni apologised, and pushed forward two chairs, and the men seated themselves. They were both in evening dress; in De Costa senior's shirt front blazed a diamond even larger than that which his son affected on such occasions.

"I may recall to you, Mr. Talham"—there was an offensive little pause before the name—"that I am engaged in the shipping trade. I sometimes send cargoes to South America"—he smiled again—"and sometimes to China."

"That is very interesting," said Talham. "I think shipping is one of the most fascinating branches of commercial endeavour."

"I am glad you think so," said the old De Costa. "Sometimes," he continued, "I find it necessary to engage a super-cargo to carry out the more delicate and intricate negotiations which are sometimes associated with the transference of the goods shipped."

Talham nodded.

"I quite understand the functions of the super-cargo," he said.

"Some years ago," the old man went on reminiscently, "I had to send rather an important cargo to one of the islands of the West Pacific." He shrugged his shoulders and waved his hands in one motion. "I cannot recall exactly where the cargo was to land, or what it consisted of; but I have a most vivid recollection of a gentleman who called upon me at my office in Little Saville Street on one occasion. And I also remember having engaged him to carry out certain duties. In so engaging him it was necessary to take him into my confidence, to an extent"—he smiled. "For instance, I had to explain that he would pick up a collier at a certain point at sea, and that he would land bales of hardware in a very difficult place."

"In the Philippines," said Talham cheerily. "And it was not hardware, but rifles, if I remember rightly."

"As to that," the other hastened to say, "I have no distinct recollection. At any rate there was an accident: my coal was stolen, my collier, which I specially chartered to meet my ship, was met by another. The coal was stolen, I repeat. Later my ship was held up by a make-believe warship, and the merchandise was removed, against the captain's wish. That Mr.—er—Talham, was piracy."

"It was piracy," admitted Talham pleasantly. "A gross act of piracy, undoubtedly."

"I am glad you agree," said De Costa.

"What would you call the act of running guns for half-breed Philippians?" asked Captain Talham.

The old man flushed. It was not the accusation which annoyed him; it was that horrid word "half-breed."

"That would not be piracy," continued Talham drily. "That would be just an act contrary to every civilised law. Yes," he said, "I am Talham. I don't need to hide it from you. What I really called myself in those days does not matter. I took your coal; I took your rifles. The rifles you were sending to niggers to enable them to shoot white men."

"Mr. Talham!" said the old man, springing to his feet.

"The rifles you were sending to niggers, I repeat," said Talham, "so that they might snipe the solitary pickets of the United States army—so that they might murder and terrorise the helpless and unarmed islanders. You're not a fool—you know the breed of the Puljanes. Why, you're one yourself!"

Talham in his insolence was a most offensive man. Tillizinni had never seen him in this mood except twice during the time he knew him.

Talham held very strong views regarding the colour question. With him a man was either black or white; he recognised no intermediary stage. Once let him depart from the pure white stock, and in Talham's eyes he might as well be coal-black. On this point he was a fanatic.

It was curious to see the old man wilt under the tall man's vitriolic tongue. It was as though he insensibly did homage in that moment to the dominant race. Despite his vast riches, despite his undoubted influence, he was a native in the presence of a white man.

Under the spell of Talham's mastery he cringed. Not so the son. He was one generation nearer whiteness. With a horrible noise which was half a scream and half a strangled cry of hatred, he leapt at the other.

Talham half turned. His hand went out rigidly. It seemed to Tillizinni that the young man did not check in his flight, but rather continued it, describing a curve about the spot where Talham stood, until he pulled up with a crash against the opposite wall. He went down in a heap.

"I'm sorry!" said Talham—but he was addressing Tillizinni.

CHAPTER 12

THE MESSAGE OF THE DEAD

IT was an embarrassing situation for Tillizinni. He saw the older man's eyes fixed on him accusingly as the youth, dazed and white, picked himself up from the floor. Yet the detective said nothing.

"You shall hear from me, Signor Tillizinni," said De Costa, senior. He spoke with deliberation, and his tone was full of menace. "Scotland Yard shall know that you consort with this adventurer, who, in addition to being a pirate, is also a common thief."

Tillizinni checked a movement of his impulsive friend with a gesture.

"A common thief?" he repeated pleasantly.

"A common thief—a burglar—who ransacked my house a fortnight ago," said De Costa. "Who cut a way through a door, and found—nothing!"

He bared his teeth in a triumphant smile.

"Here!" He thrust his hand into the inside pocket of his coat and pulled out a short bladed knife, protected by a leather sheath.

"The burglar left this behind on a desk he had forced," he said. "You will observe, Ned, that your initials are on the blade—N.T.—Ned Talham!"

Tillizinni smiled as the old man replaced the knife and made for the door.

"Yet another fact to lay before Scotland Yard," he said pleasantly, as he opened the door for the angry pair. "N.T. also stands for Nicholos Tillizinni."

The son had reached the landing, and De Costa was passing through the doorway to follow the waiting servant. At Tillizinni's words he turned.

"You?" he asked.

Tillizinni bowed.

"I came searching for a certain document stolen from the Chinese Embassy," he said. "Would you allow your son to wait in another room whilst I tell you something?"

De Costa paused irresolutely.

He walked to the door.

"You may wait downstairs for me," he said.

He came back and closed the door after him. Tillizinni strolled to the other end of the room, his hands in his pockets, his dark brow puckered in a thoughtful frown. He strolled back to meet De Costa.

"Won't you sit down?" he said, but the old man made no move.

"As I said, I went to your house—burgled it if you will—it is one of the crimes which I permit myself. I came to seek a certain dossier containing a document which I had every reason to believe was in your possession."

"You found nothing?" said the old man steadily.

"I found nothing," agreed Tillizinni. "At any rate, I did not find that which I set forth to find. What I did discover, however, was rather interesting. It was that you had at least three visitors on that night, and that they had all been Chinamen, and that one, and the most important of these"—he spoke slowly—"was quite in ignorance as to the visit of the others."

Not a muscle of the old man's face moved.

"Go on," he said.

Tillizinni had picked up a fountain pen from the desk and was pointing his remarks with little flourishes which were peculiarly his.

"Well," he began, and stopped with an exclamation of apology, for from the waving fountain-pen a few drops had fallen upon the white shirt-front of the visitor.

He stepped forward impulsively with his handkerchief and wiped them clean.

De Costa was in some doubt as to whether he should reject such civility. Then Tillizinni resumed.

"The presence of the two men was rather a mystery. I found no indication that they had stayed any time, and I gathered by the fact that you had written very elaborate directions, that they had come to consult you as to the best method of getting out of England."

Still the man made no sign.

"You had carefully written—possibly on two half-sheets of notepaper, since I found the corresponding halves with the tell-tale address upon them in the wastepaper basket—a string of names of places written in English and blotted on a fairly clean pad. Since those names occur twice I gathered there was some slight difference between them, and I gather that you had advised them to take different routes.

"One went by way of Ostend to Petrograd, Moscow, and Tomsk, and *viâ* the Trans-Siberian Railway; the other was apparently advised to leave by way of Liverpool on a Chinese cargo boat which sailed this morning. This much I gathered from the fact that you had given him the name of an agent in Liverpool to whom he could apply. That also you very indiscreetly blotted."

The old man's face was livid now.

"And what do you make of all this?" he asked with a show of bravado.

"As far as I can understand," said Tillizinni, "two men in your pay are responsible for the abstraction of a very important document from the Chinese

Embassy. Piecing the story together I understand that you are in agreement with Soo, a scholarly gentleman and a mutual acquaintance."

He bowed ironically.

"At the last moment, or possibly long before the last moment, you feared that Soo would play you false, and went behind his back to bribe two hirelings to deliver what was found to you. Possibly you did not see the workings of the Chinese mind, nor foresee the tragedy which must inevitably occur when one member of the party engaged to rob the ambassador happens to be the brother of your defrauded partner."

"The brother!"

De Costa was shocked, he was terrified; they read that in his eyes.

Tillizinni nodded.

"The brother," he repeated, "of Ts'i Soo was the unfortunate man who was found doubled up in the bureau of the ambassador's study. As I say, you probably did not foresee this unpleasant ending to the adventure, and went into it with no more idea than of being party to a minor felony. Your men killed the Chinaman who called himself 'Star above the Yamen' because they saw no other way of silencing him. They brought the documents straight on to you."

"That is a lie!" said De Costa.

"They brought the documents to you," repeated Tillizinni, "and they have never left you day or night."

He took a step closer to De Costa, and the old man shrunk back. His hands went up to his right breast.

"They are probably in an inside pocket of your waistcoat," said Tillizinni. "May I see?"

He reached out his hand, but before he could touch him the old man turned with a snarl, dashed open the door, and swung himself through it, descending the steps at a pace which did credit to his age, but was disastrous to his dignity.

Tillizinni laughed. He sat back in his chair and laughed that silent chuckle of his for fully three minutes.

"But why—why," protested Talham, "why not have taken the papers whilst you could? For heaven's sake, why did you let him go?"

Tillizinni shook his head.

"I could not take the document from him," he said with a smile, "because I had already taken it when I was wiping his shirt front," and he laid on the table a thin folded sheet closely written in Chinese characters.

Very slowly Talham read:

"Chu, Mi, Tsan Sui, and Tulm, ... together .... as brothers, swearing .... This we say, being mechanical men from divers provinces brought together, because of our great skill, to the shadow of the Emperor's house (here was something indecipherable) that we shall finish the tomb, fitting bronze doors, also working on a machine which the philosopher made.

"One of us to the other said—if the Emperor be buried and with him mighty treasures, how easy will it be for us—we shall know all the mechanical secrets of this place—to find a means for returning, and, if there be treasure buried, to take it away with us; and we agreed. So we have set this down for the guidance of our sons if we be dead when the great attempt shall be made, that the bronze door which shall fall at the entrance, and may not be lifted except with the strength of fifty bullocks—and the .... be taken away.

"We have made a pit so large as the door itself, and there is nothing solid beneath that floor; so that if you shall find at either side of the entrance, between two great rocks carved two bronze images buried the length of a finger, between stones, you shall pull these and the door will fall as it fell before, but never to be raised, save with the strength of fifty bullocks.

"And inside is a large cave with two silver lamps which shall burn on the day of its closing, and from one of these lamps there is a long chain of bronze which runs through a tunnel along the roof, and is mechanically connected (here again the manuscript is indecipherable).

"If you shall pull upon the silver lamp which is nearest the door of bronze, the whole of the door of silver which is at the foot of the steps shall open. I myself made this tunnel and placed the chain therein, fixing with mechanical contrivance.

"Beware of all steps save the spirit steps, for they are devilishly made by..............

"Inside the silver door you shall find the great rivers working marvellously, and on the roof of the cave, which has been made smooth with great labour, many stars shaped .... precious stones. And here will the Emperor be laid—he and his wives, and in a pit which we have dug on either side shall be cast the ornaments of gold and silver, and the jewels which he wore in his lifetime, and the jewels also of his wives and of his blood relations.

"Let our memories be blessed by our children, that we have brought fortune to them, and made them richer than kings, and given them dominions greater than the provinces of the barbarians."

Talham read these documents through twice, scribbling in his angular writing a rough translation the first time and amending as he read it again.

He looked up at the detective.

Tillizinni had been infected with something of the fever which possessed the other.

"What do you think?" asked Talham.

"I think it is a wonderful discovery," said Tillizinni, and he meant it, for that document to him was as precious as anything which Talham might secure from the vaults beneath Mount Li.

It was written on paper of extraordinary texture. Indeed, it was as thin as that quality which is known as "Indian paper" to-day.

Very few of the characters had been damaged, and such obliterations as there were, were caused by the folds in the document.

Talham looked up with a puzzled frown.

"Still, this tells us nothing as to the locality of the mountain?" he said.

Tillizinni shook his head.

"Curiously, I have never thought that the locality was ever likely to be established," he said. "Probably the Chinese ambassador referred to the locality of the tomb rather than the exact geographical position of the mountain.

"I have been looking through some books in the British Museum," he said, "and it appears that the Emperor had expressed a desire to be buried in the land of his birth. As you knew, he was practically a usurper of the Chinese throne. The Empire as we know it to-day had no existence until he brought the provinces together into a united whole. He was a sort of prehistoric Bismarck."

"I have thought of that, too," said Talham. "The old kingdom of Ts'in was situated in a rough circle, of which the town of Hoo Sin is the centre. It is obviously not the Mount Li in the neighbourhood of Pekin."

There was a long silence; which Talham broke.

"Delay," he said, "is repugnant to the active mind; action is the essence of vitality. Seconds, strenuously saved at one end, are lessened hours of peace at the other."

"When you have finished delivering these excellent maxims," said Tillizinni with a faint smile, "perhaps you will come to the point."

"My point is this," said Talham shortly; "we must go along and find that tomb before somebody else discovers it. You see, we have the information which was denied to De Costa and to his confederates—the information contained in the jade bracelet."

"We?" said Tillizinni, raising his eyebrows.

"We," said Talham calmly. "You have been so kind to me, and have offered me such hospitality, even going so far to advance me the small sums which were necessary to my sustenance. No, no," he went on, for Tillizinni would have hushed him down, "these matters, material as they are, show the tendencies of a soul. I once thought," he mused, but Tillizinni cut him short.

The orations of Captain Talham were inclined to err on the side of longevity, and Tillizinni regarded himself as more or less ephemeral.

Besides which, Tillizinni had work to do, a description of Soo had been circulated up and down the country, and every haunt which might shelter him had been systematically searched. The ports were being watched, and no Chinaman went on board an ocean-going liner without first passing the strict scrutiny of detectives who were watching the outgoing steamers. In spite of this fact no trace of the man could be found.

Neither Talham nor Tillizinni agreed with the theory that he had been drowned in his attempt to escape, and Talham, who invariably held stronger views than most men, and expressed them with greater strength, even went so far as to accompany the dragging parties on the banks of the canal, and at intervals to deliver little speeches on the futility of vain effort—an embarrassing situation from which Tillizinni delivered the searchers by the exercise of his tact.

By Tillizinni's instructions, the house in Curzon Street was watched day and night. He had no illusions, he knew full well that if Soo could strike a blow at Talham through the girl, he would do so.

The newspapers had arisen to the occasion and had referred exultantly to the "bottling up" of the fugitive Chinaman. It was a little phrase coined in a hurried moment which caught the fancy of the great public; the "bottling up" of England to hold an escaping murderer, appealed to the popular imagination.

Curiously enough, the greatest difficulty had been found in identifying Soo with any known person in China. The Governor of Tai-pan, with whom the Chinaman claimed relationship, had telegraphed to his Government that his only son was pursuing his studies in Nanking, and could not possibly be the wanted man.

Nevertheless, though the Chinese Government had promised every assistance to bring the culprit to justice, and to thoroughly punish him if he reached Chinese territory, Tillizinni knew that it was for China that the man would make.

Talham had gone home, and the precious document had been locked in Tillizinni's safe, and he himself was preparing for a greatly-needed night's rest, when his sleepy servant brought a plain envelope addressed to the detective.

"How did this come?" asked Tillizinni.

"By a little boy, sir," said the man.

Tillizinni held the envelope to the light. It showed nothing more sinister than a folded sheet of paper, and he slit it open. There were only a few words, but those words were particularly interesting.

The letter was without superscription, and ran:

"Some day I will 'bottle up' somebody who is very precious to your friend, and you may be sure that when she is once again in my hands, nothing you can do will save her."

Tillizinni re-read the letter and sent for the messenger.

The boy could tell him little, except that a man had given the letter to him to deliver, and since the description of that man did not in any way tally with the description of Soo, Tillizinni gathered that the messenger originally sent, had chosen a deputy, for reasons of his own.

He sent the boy away, read the letter for the third time, and after telephoning to assure himself that the guards he had fixed in Curzon Street were at their posts, he went to bed and slept as soundly as any man could sleep who had not closed his eyes in slumber for forty-eight hours.

It was broad daylight when his servant brought him in his chocolate and toast. With it came one of the few letters which were addressed personally to him. It was from Yvonne Yale, a charming little note of thanks for the service he had rendered, but she made no mention of Talham.

Tillizinni smiled.

Now that the excitement had passed, and the exhilaration of the rescue subsided, he imagined that the girl might very properly blame Talham for the part he had played. In this he was wrong, as he was to discover.

He spent the whole of the day at Scotland Yard in the laboratory, making experiments to demonstrate the value of a new finger-print method.

He did not see Talham that night, nor the next day either, for the matter of that, but on the third day following the discovery of the paper, and the fourth after the abduction of the girl, Talham came to see him in a state of great excitement.

"Soo is in London," he said briefly, and seemed pleased with himself that he could report information to the encyclopædia detective.

Tillizinni nodded.

"I know that," he said.

"What is more," said Talham, "I've been followed about for the last two days by a couple of men. I tried to lure them into a dark court last night to beat them up."

"I'm very glad you didn't," said Tillizinni drily, "because those were eminently respectable members of the Metropolitan Police, whom I have put on to protect you from whatever harm might be coming to you."

Talham looked a little crestfallen. He had come prepared to accept a little praise from the other for his acumen and his powers of perception.

"But how do you know that Soo is in London?" asked Tillizinni.

"Because I saw him," said the calm Talham, and secured his sensation.

Tillizinni raised his eyebrows.

"Saw him and did not arrest him?"

"It was rather difficult," explained Talham. "I was on the platform of a tube station at Piccadilly Circus just as the train was moving out. In a rear carriage as it went past me, gathering speed at every second, I saw a man whom I'll swear was Soo, with a perfectly fitting beard. I know him, moreover, by the scar above his left eye. Just as he came abreast of me he raised his eyes, and then I was sure. I couldn't stop the train—which reminds me," he said portentously, "that I must report the station-master and several of the employées on the Underground Railway for marked insolence."

Tillizinni gathered that Talham had made himself objectionable, and sympathised with the station officials.

"I couldn't telephone through to the next station, and if I had, I probably should not have got through in time," he said, "and if I got through——"

"Anyway, you didn't telephone at all," said Tillizinni with a smile, "and he alighted at the next station, and disappeared."

Talham nodded.

"I have known he's been in London for some days," said Tillizinni. "As a matter of fact, there is nothing very clever in finding that out, because I received a note which was unmistakably from him. Scotland Yard can do no more than they are doing, and unless he leaves in an aeroplane, and we have made provision for that contingency, I don't see how he is to escape from England."

Tillizinni had applied for leave, he told the other, and was prepared to leave for China the following week. If he had expected Talham to be excited or elated or in any way pleasantly surprised, he was doomed to disappointment.

Talham had taken it for granted that Tillizinni, despite all his multifarious interests, would grasp the opportunity to visit the Celestial Kingdom and enjoy the adventure which his enterprise promised.

"Everything, of course, depends upon what happens to Soo," the detective went on. "I can't leave if he's arrested, I can't leave if he's not arrested. Our only hope for my holiday is that Soo, in some mysterious fashion which is peculiarly his, makes his escape from this country."

As a matter of fact, the detective did not leave that week nor the next, nor that which followed.

On the Saturday of the third week came a letter; it bore the postmark of Madison Square Gardens post-office, and was in the handwriting of Soo. It was brief, and reiterated the threat which he had uttered in his shorter epistle, but more specifically, in language which need not be repeated nor transcribed.

Tillizinni locked it away with the other documents affecting the case and prepared for his departure.

* * * *

There was one man as interested in the movement of Soo as Tillizinni.

Old Raymond de Costa, a bitter and hateful man, and also a fearful man. He dreaded the law on the one side, and the vengeance of Soo on the other, if it ever came out that it was he who had played him false.

The news published in the morning papers that Soo had reached America came as a great relief to the old man; it freed him to pursue his private feud against Tillizinni and his insufferable friend.

He discovered the loss of the document for which he had sacrificed so much, yet did not associate the detective with the theft until his valet drew attention to the ink-spot on the dress shirt which came back from the laundry.

"You've had some ink on your shirt, sir," said the man.

With a scowl De Costa remembered the circumstances under which it had been acquired.

"Yes, throw it away," he said shortly.

The man folded up the garment with a little smile.

De Costa detected it, and turned on him the vials of his vitriolic wrath.

"I'm very sorry, sir," said the man apologetically. "I wasn't smiling at the shirt, I was just remembering how a gentleman I once valeted was robbed of fifty pounds."

"I don't want to hear about it," growled the old man.

Then curiosity got the better of him.

"I suppose you're aching to tell me," he said ungraciously. "How was it?"

"It happened in the West End," said the valet. "A man was writing a note with a fountain-pen in the vestibule of one of the cafés. He happened to shake it, and some drops fell on the gentleman's shirt. The gentleman who did it was very sorry and wiped it off with his own silk handkerchief, but my master lost a bundle of notes from the inside pocket of his coat whilst the wiping process was going on."

As he proceeded, De Costa's face was a study. He realised now how the paper came to be lost.

So Tillizinni had the paper, and had, too, evidence as to his complicity in the Embassy robbery! But had he? Nobody would be able to identify the documents which were stolen. It had been stated so at the inquest.

No, there would be no evidence to convict the respectable Raymond de Costa in that, or he would have been arrested by now. Besides, he was a known antiquarian and a collector of Chinese objects, art, and literature. There would be every excuse for his being in possession of such a thing. He had the transcription, and the document had no value now save to the antiquarian.

He must act at once.

CHAPTER 13

CAPTAIN TALHAM PROPOSES

TALHAM had proposed to Yvonne Yale. It had followed many meetings, many calls at the house in Upper Curzon Street, many lengthy orations on the future of applied mechanics delivered to Mrs. Yale, who took what might be termed a shareholder's interest in such matters, and the end of it was that Talham, after a sleepless night, called upon the Yales at five o'clock in the morning.

This statement is made in all seriousness, because it is true. At this outrageous hour Captain Talham, a tall, handsome figure of a man, tanned and debonair, knocked at the door of the Yale ménage.

He had knocked half a dozen times before the shuffling of slippered feet told him that his efforts had succeeded. A sleepy servant admitted him, albeit reluctantly. She asked him to stand in the hall while she went to arouse her mistress.

"Remember," said Talham, solemnly, "that it is only Miss Yvonne that I wish to see."

The servant came down again in her wrapper and led him to the drawing-room.

Talham, with deplorable familiarity, pulled the blinds up.

In five minutes the girl came in. She wore a long kimono of dark blue, edged with Russian embroidery, and she had hidden the glory of her hair under a boudoir cap.

She looked singularly beautiful—he had never seen her more so.

She was worried, too. Naturally, she could only interpret this unexpected call into a recurrence of the perils which she had already experienced.

"I have called to see you, Miss Yale," said Talham, gravely, "on a most important matter." She nodded and waited.

"Last night, or, rather, in the early hours of this morning, I had an interview with a Mr. de Costa," said Talham.

He went on to give particulars of that interview. She seemed more than ordinarily interested. It was rather as though she were eager for all he could tell her. The light of sympathy was in her eyes. She sat on one of those hard, straight-backed chairs which are to be found in London drawing-rooms, and are designed to discourage lengthy visits, her hands clasping her crossed knees, as step by step, concealing nothing, exaggerating nothing, omitting nothing—except, perhaps, his own foresight and resourcefulness—Talham took her through the act of his "just piracy," as he described it. He went on to tell the full story of the Emperor's tomb. When he had finished, there was a pause. Then she said gently:

"I understand, Captain Talham, and I appreciate your confidence. I am glad you have told me, because Mr. de Costa himself sent me a version last night which was not as complimentary to yourself as you have made it." She frowned a little as at some unpleasant memory. De Costa had threatened her—she did not tell him this. Now, in a panic, she realised that the information for which the old man had asked and which she had not at the moment possessed, was now hers!

"Why, oh why, have you come?" she asked.

"You are entitled to know that," said Talham. "I must hurry forward all my arrangements and go back to China. I cannot go back until I know one thing. I cannot wait a day," he said, vehemently, "with one doubt in my mind. Miss Yale——"

He leant forward, his hands tightly clasped, his face tense and drawn, a new Talham, and a Talham she had never seen before—the strong, clean soul of the man shone in his face.

"I want a partner," he said. "I want—you!"

He jerked the last word.

She rose slowly, and looked down at him still in the same attitude in which he had made his plea—and a look of pity and something else came over her face.

"I am sorry, Captain Talham," she said in a low voice. "I cannot agree, though I recognise how great an honour you have done me."

He got up and drew a long breath.

"You cannot agree," he repeated.

She did not trust herself to speak, but shook her head slowly.

Then a pause—one of those seemingly interminable pauses so trying to the nerves. Neither of the two spoke. Talham's eyes were on the floor; hers, filled with pity, were on his face. It seemed that five minutes passed like this, though, as a matter of fact, the period was less.

Then Talham said, "Oh!"

That was all he said. It was not an "Oh" of pain, or an "Oh" of surprise, or "Oh" of indifference; it was just "Oh!"

When Talham left the house that memorable morning to return to the hotel after his fantastic and fruitless quest, Yvonne Yale sat for quite a long time in the little drawing-room.

It was not an apartment which shone in the merciless grey light of early morning. At such an hour you saw the mark of the cleaner's vacuum-brush—the discolourations where an amateur varnisher had endeavoured to renovate the chipped chairs—the thinness of the carpet here and there, and, most appalling of all, the blatant artificiality of the "Gloire de Dijon" roses which Mrs. Yale had brought back from Ostend with her the previous year.

Yvonne had taken a seat by the window and was sitting on it sideways, one arm thrown across the back and the other twisting and untwisting a piece of loose embroidery upon her kimono.

She was thankful, at that moment, that her mother was a heavy sleeper and had not been aroused by the summons.

Yvonne Yale hoped that she was a dutiful daughter. There were times when she came perilously near being glad that she was not. This was a moment when the presence of her mother would have sent her to her room.

It was good to be here alone, in the silence and in the sweet light of the early day, to think this problem over—for Talham had become a problem.

A fortnight ago, she would have dismissed his proposal with a laugh—and found relief in the sight of his disappearing back.

But now, this tall, brown man, with his obvious sincerity, his interminable speeches, his earnestness, which verged upon pomposity, had taken a place with her.

He filled a niche no other man had occupied, could occupy, to do Talham justice, for Nature does not create duplicates of his quality.

Exactly where was that niche? This speculation puzzled her. If she could have answered that question after long deliberation and self-analysis, the problem was a problem no longer.

Where did he stand? At that moment of time she had no feeling of love, as young people understand love, no quickening of the pulse at his approach, no blotting out of her soul's sun at his departure—no gnawing ache or unsatisfied voidance of soul at his continued absence.

Indeed, she had none of the conventional symptoms, and might be excused the belief that, so far as love was concerned, there was no bond between Talham and her.

And yet——

She walked to the French windows and, opening them, stepped out on to the little stone balcony. She looked up and down the street; there was nobody in sight; it would be little short of a social crime for any of the inhabitants of Upper Curzon Street to be seen abroad at that hour, save in evening dress.

Insensibly, she found herself looking long, and a little wistfully, in the direction which she knew Talham must have taken.

He was something more to her than a friend, though he was not even a friend in the accepted sense. The confidences, which mark the growth of friendship, had been all one-sided. It had been Talham who had talked—be sure of that. She had listened excellently.

Talham's passion was an inspiration, a thing born of a momentary glance—love at first sight, though the term is hateful.

To fulfil the requirements of the ideal, those two souls should have leapt together to light, as two chemical elements dormant apart, will, on impact, forsake their independent properties and mingle riotously in the creation of a newer element.

But Talham had done all the leaping. The girl had been but the passive agent, a screen to reflect his brilliancy—Talham was a dazzling searchlight that played on Yvonne Yale. She, herself, produced no increase in the power of illumination.

It was absurd to say that she was cold. All women are cold—just as all men are liars. In a dark room a diamond is undistinguishable from half a brick. People who, when groping in the gloom of ignorance, in a vain search for the furnace, which they felt must burn within the heart of the girl, not infrequently came up against the refrigerating plant, and retired in disorder, composing wicked little epigrams.

She stood for a long time on the balcony—then returned to the room.

The servant, who had admitted her, still waited resentfully. Her name was Martha Ann, and she had in her colourless composition no romance. Her hour for rising was seven, and she had risen at five. That was all.

"Do you want me, miss?" she asked, with offensive patience.

Yvonne shook her head, and the girl went off.

"I don't suppose I shall get to sleep now," she said bitterly. "A nice time in the morning for a gentleman to call."

She said many other things, but was careful to wait until her voice was only represented to the girl below by a succession of incomprehensible sounds, the tenor of which might be grasped from the fact that each sentence ended on a high note.

When Martha came down at the conventional hour she found her young mistress fully dressed, moreover, dressed for the street.

"I am going to Covent Garden to buy some flowers, Martha," said Yvonne.

Martha tightened her lips and said nothing until she heard the door close behind the girl.

"What a house!" said Martha, and raised her eyes to the ceiling.

It was a glorious morning. The air was sweet and clean; the flood of golden sunlight which bathed the green spaces of the city squares and made ornate avenues of the long orderly streets, was a veritable elixir of life.

There was a spring even in the hard, asphalt pavement that morning, and the girl found herself singing quietly to herself as she walked along.

Covent Garden Market was no great distance from the hotel which housed Talham. An hour later she was standing in the Strand, her arms filled with dewy blooms, looking with a thoughtful eye upon the great block of buildings which constituted the caravanserai.

Breakfast was seldom a pleasant meal in Upper Curzon Street. The urbanity, the graciousness, and the Foreign Office manner of Mrs. Yale were never on view at so early an hour. The great hostess of eleven p.m. became the vinegary housekeeper of nine a.m.

It was as though Nature had reversed her processes, and had evolved from the overnight butterfly a most business-like grub.

There was a pile of letters by the side of Mrs. Yale's plate when she came down to breakfast. Yvonne had already begun her meal, and the elder woman gave her a slight peck in the region between the eye and the *superior maxilla*, which signified the automatic continuance of her devotion.

She flounced into her chair, unfolded her napkin, glanced at her papers, and criticised the bacon at one and the same time.

Yvonne glanced at her idly. Instinctively, she had closed all the sound-proof doors of her mind on her stepmother's entrance.

"Bills," said Mrs. Yale grimly. "We shall have to draw in our horns."

Yvonne had never completely satisfied herself as to what were the horns to which Mrs. Yale invariably referred. If it was the cornucopian horn, it was generally drawn in empty.

"Here's this exasperating broker of mine," said the elder woman, looking at a long statement of account. "I told him particularly not to sell Long Island Gas until it reached eighty-four—and here he has sold it at eighty-one!"

"It is now seventy-six," said Yvonne, drily. "If you had waited for your eighty-four you might have lost much more money."

She had taken to a study of the Share Market and its report from sheer self-defence.

Mrs. Yale opened another letter. It was very short and, apparently, unpleasant.

"Good heavens!" said she.

Her language at breakfast was generally violent. It was, in a sense, an act of devotion, since it had been acquired from her militant husband, who long since had carried his sword to heaven.

"What is the matter? From the bank?" asked Yvonne.

Mrs. Yale invariably kept her most violent expletives for the bank.

"He says I am eighty pounds overdrawn—will I put this right at once!"

Mrs. Yale glared at her unoffending stepdaughter.

"It's absurd," she said, "ridiculous! Eighty pounds overdrawn! Why, I've never heard of such a thing in my life."

Yvonne smiled. She, at any rate, had had this experience before.

"I know what it is," said Mrs. Yale, with sudden decision. "They've got one of those wretched horse-racing bank clerks who is robbing the bank. He's filching my account because he knows I am so careless. I suspected it all along!"

"The last time, mother," said Yvonne quietly, "you thought Martha had been using your blank cheques. Why don't you fill up your counterfoils, and then you would know how much money you had?"

Mrs. Yale offered no reply. She made a further rapid survey of the morning's post without finding satisfaction. She reserved two obviously private letters for the last. These she opened and read carefully. Then she folded them up, placed them in their envelopes, and slipped them into a bag which hung at her side—for all the world like a sabretache.

She scrutinised Yvonne with a long and approving scrutiny.

"My dear," she said finally, "you've got to make a good marriage."

"Have I?" said the girl coolly. "I thought only people in novelettes made good marriages. What do you mean by making a good marriage, exactly?"

"Now, don't be tiresome, Yvonne," said Mrs. Yale. "I've been a good mother to you. I've done my best to bring around you the most eligible men in London. I've spent money like water—which reminds me, we shall have to have that kitchen range seen to; Martha tells me it's smoking again, and she can't get the oven hot. Where was I?—Oh, I was saying, I have spent money like water, and I think I am entitled to some return. Not," she hastened to say, "that I expect any monetary reward for my sacrifices——"

Yvonne had heard all this before. In one form or another this conversation was almost a daily feature of her life.

"I can't help thinking, my dear," said Mrs. Yale, putting her head on one side and looking at her stepdaughter with her pale blue eyes opened to their widest extent. "I cannot help thinking that you have not always appreciated my efforts. That new dress, for instance, which I bought at the summer sales—you have never worn it."

"It's totally unsuitable for me, mother," said Yvonne. "I thought I told you so. It's not the kind of dress that I should care to be seen walking in. I'd always much rather choose my own."

"That's pique," said her stepmother. "That's naughty pique."

Yvonne made no reply. It was useless to argue the point.

"Then, the other night, when Mr. de Costa called to congratulate you on your rescue from those horrid China people"—Yvonne's lips curled scornfully—"you came down absolutely without a jewel on. Yet, in your room, on your own table, for you to wear, are my own pearls—my own bangles."

Yvonne smiled.

"My dear mother," she said, "I will not wear imitation pearls, even to please you, and most certainly I will not wear any kind of jewel which everybody, who is in the habit of coming to this house, has seen round your neck at least a dozen times. You see they are rather unmistakable," she said carefully. "If they were real, they could not be worth less than fifty thousand pounds."

"There is a certain finesse in these things," said Mrs. Yale vaguely; but she did not pursue the topic.

She waited until her own meal was nearly at an end, and the girl was folding her serviette preparatory to leaving the table, before she returned to the attack.

"What about young De Costa?" she asked.

"What about him?"

"Has he proposed to you?"

"I really forget," said Yvonne carelessly. "These people do propose in a way—almost mechanically. I don't like him—he is rather a worm."

Mrs. Yale frowned.

"A most unkind description," she said severely. "His father is immensely rich. He gave you a beautiful bangle which I never see you wearing, by the way." She paused for an explanation, but Yvonne offered none. "And what of Captain Talham?"

Yvonne rose from the table.

"I don't propose to discuss these matters at breakfast, mother," she said. "You know, it takes all the romance out of a thing. It reduces love and marriage to the level of cold bacon."

"But has he?" persisted Mrs. Yale.

"Has he what?" the girl evaded.

"Has he proposed to you, my dear? Let me impress upon you this fact—that though Captain Talham is not enormously wealthy, he has prospects, and he is enormously generous. I hope you have not forgotten the fact that he rescued you from the hands of those terrible persons."

"He has proposed," interrupted the girl, "if that is what you mean. In fact, he called this morning at five o'clock to make his proposal."

CHAPTER 14

AND RECEIVES HIS ANSWER

MRS. YALE gasped.

"Proposed this morning!" she repeated incredulously. "At five o'clock!"

"He called at five this morning," said the girl, "as Martha Ann will tell you, if you have any doubts."

"Why was I not aroused?" asked Mrs. Yale, with a sense of grievance that she had missed something.

"Because he wasn't proposing to you," said the girl calmly. "It was my affair entirely."

Mrs. Yale got up from the table, a little hurt.

"I think, Yvonne," she said, with a sort of stagey gentleness, "that you might remember my anxieties and sacrifices."

"I do not forget them," said her stepdaughter; "only, unfortunately, this is my anxiety and my sacrifice."

Mrs. Yale sniffed, and searched aimlessly for her handkerchief, but thought better of it. After all, Yvonne was not the sort of girl to be moved by tears. She did not need to have this fact again impressed upon her. She was hard. The dear colonel, her father, had shown similar callousness of tears, and had laid down the perfectly dreadful theory that the more one wept the less one perspired. And indeed, he had written a paper on the subject, and had invited the Royal Society to allow him to read it—a request which was respectfully declined.

The subject of her marriage, as Yvonne had so truly said, had formed a periodic matter for argument—only unfortunately, in the present instance, it was absolutely necessary that Mrs. Yale should know where she stood.

She had hinted as much—indeed, had said as much—before; but now she could say so in very truth. The eccentric behaviour of Long Island Gas was as nothing to the monstrous conduct of an oil well in Southern Russia.

Quite a lot of Mrs. Yale's money had gone from time to time towards the sinking of a bore hole upon what the directors invariably and carefully referred to as "The Property."

When they wrote to Mrs. Yale they referred to themselves as "Your Directors." It gave the good lady the comforting feeling that they were distant relations—though what satisfaction accrued to her from that, Heaven only knows.

"Your Directors," who had started out on their career joyful and optimistic, making conservative estimate of future profits, which were beyond the dreams of avarice, had grown rather gloomy of late. "Your Directors" had been probing the bowels of the earth without any great profit to themselves, and apparently without any great inconvenience to the earth. The oil, in its furtive, sneaking way, seemed to have got wind of "Your Directors'" intentions, and moved off to a neighbouring oil field.

"Your Directors"—sharp and cunning fellows—were not to be evaded. They purchased the neighbouring oil field, and told Mrs. Yale, by private letter, that the prospects were of the brightest, and they hoped soon to make a definite statement.

After six months they made a definite statement—but the prospects were no longer of the brightest. The oil, in a panic, had retired some thirty versts.

"Your Directors" were considering their position. Mrs. Yale was impressed by the whole-hearted devotion of "Your Directors" to her interests, and the employment of the blessed word "versts" brightened her up. After all, it looked as if there was a mine somewhere, and undoubtedly it was in a foreign country where "miles" had a special name of their own, and so many other extraordinary things happened.

In one way or another, as a result of poetic folders and disinterested advice from Mr. Macdougal and other outside brokers with names reminiscent of the Old Testament, Mrs. Yale had lost some eight hundred pounds; not a considerable sum to most of the people who lived in Upper Curzon Street, and not one to bother even a woman circumstanced as Mrs. Yale was—the morning after the loss.

Yvonne knew nothing of her stepmother's folly, or she would have worried much more than did Mrs. Yale. As a matter of fact, that amiable lady did not greatly distress herself. She was obsessed with the idea that she was a born financier. She adjusted things. She had learnt the financier's trick—which is, not to borrow from Peter to pay Paul, but to borrow from Peter, pay half of Paul's demands, and utilise the other half for playing margin on sure enough stock.

In this way the debt both to Peter and Paul may be discharged with a bit of luck, and anyway Paul has had something on account.

Mrs. Yale spent the day shopping pleasantly; Yvonne dreamt away the hours in reverie. She thought of Talham, that first meeting in the park, the adventures that followed her parting with the jade bracelet, and all he had said that morning. She acted on a sudden impulse and sent him a wire.

So the day wore on, bringing Mrs. Yale back from her precious bargain sales, weary but triumphant, and the possessor of many articles for which she had no particular use, but which were undeniably cheap.

Just before dinner the second visitor was announced.

Yvonne read the card and frowned. "Mr. Raymond de Costa," said the pasteboard elaborately. He had called for an answer to his letter.

It was not the hour that visitors usually called, unless they were invited to dinner, and, as Martha Ann can testify, the dinner that night was of significant frugality. Mrs. Yale, dining alone (and it was tantamount to dining alone when she had no other companion at the table but her stepdaughter), was an exponent of the simple life.

Martha Ann ushered the visitor into the drawing-room, then flew to find Mrs. Yale, to warn her that three chops and a pint of dessicated soup was very poor preparation for a dinner-party, if it were to include Mr. de Costa.

Yvonne was dressing, but came down within a few minutes of his arrival. The old man rose and favoured her with a bow as she came in.

"I have called for your answer, Miss Yale," said De Costa.

"I have no answer to give you now, that I was not prepared to give you yesterday," said the girl, quietly. "I could not, even if I knew, put you in possession of the information you require."

De Costa shrugged his shoulders.

"It means such a lot to you," he said, "and to your mother. I am sure she would persuade you——"

"My mother could not persuade me to do anything I thought was dishonourable and unworthy," she replied, with a note of hauteur in her voice.

"You know the consequences?" asked the old man.

"I know what you threaten," said the girl, steadily. "That you will have Captain Talham arrested, and that you will subpœna me, and force me to tell you what was inscribed on the bracelet."

The old man nodded.

"Yes," he said, "that is my intention. You can save your friend a lot of trouble, and save me a great deal of inconvenience, by telling me all you know."

She was silent.

"By hook or by crook, I am going to learn what you have to tell," said De Costa savagely. "This man has done me a grievous wrong, and I intend repaying myself for all the inconvenience to which he has put me, and for all the money which I have lost as a result of his act of theft. The bracelet was not yours; it is not his."

"There is no Court of Law in England that would force me to say what I did not wish to say," she said firmly. "Legally—however unfortunate it was your son should have given it to me—it was mine. It is now out of my hands. I cannot tell you anything about it without Captain Talham's permission."

De Costa shrugged.

"Your refusal to answer will be accepted as an answer unfavourable to the prisoner. If you lie, the judges and the jury will know."

"Have no fear," she said haughtily. "I shall not say anything which is not true."

It was at that tense moment that Mrs. Yale came in. She boasted her ability to take in a situation at a glance. Now she sought to justify that boast.

"Ah!" she said pleasantly, with a genial smile which comprehended both the old man and her stepdaughter. "I see you have succeeded in persuading my obstinate daughter."

"I have not yet, madam," said De Costa, putting on his mask of courtesy. "I do not doubt we shall succeed eventually," he added, with a smile. "I have had to take a very serious line with Miss Yale, and I know that you will support me in my action."

"You may be sure, Mr. de Costa," said the lady fervently, "that whatever action you take you have the approval of one who is not only a fond and doting mother, but is also sufficiently a woman of the world to realise the disinterestedness of your action."

It was a speech almost worthy of Talham. She turned to the girl.

"Yvonne," she said, with proper sadness, "I have never yet exercised that authority which my position and my age and the regard in which I was held by that hero who has long since carried his sword to Heaven"—she dabbed her eyes automatically—"entitles me. Yet I feel," she said firmly, as she drew herself erect as a queen-mother would draw herself erect, "that I must, in this present instance, insist upon your taking a certain line of conduct—a line of conduct which will be beneficial to us all, and which will be creditable and worthy of the name you bear. Mr. de Costa has honoured me with his confidence."

There was a little exchange of bows between the two.

"He has told me what steps he would take in certain eventualities. For the honour of the house——!" She laid her hand with dramatic effect on the girl's shoulder.

Yvonne heaved a deep sigh. She put up her hand and took that of her mother's. It was not so much to demonstrate her affection as to relieve an intolerable, melodramatic situation.

"There is no profit in talking to me like that, mother," she said quietly. "You do not help me or help Mr. de Costa. The honour of the house, you may be sure, is safely in my keeping," she said, with her little chin tilted upward proudly. "It is indeed more in my keeping than it is in yours."

"But think of the court; think of the newspapers!" wailed Mrs. Yale. "Think of the scandal!"

"I have thought of all that," said Yvonne with a little smile. "I do not relish the prospect any more than you. If Mr. de Costa does this disgraceful thing," she shrugged her shoulders, "what else can I do but endure? Under any circumstances"—she faced the old man squarely—"I will not tell you what I know about Captain Talham's plans."

The opposition he was encountering had fanned the fury of the old man to a white heat of rage. The veins in his forehead were swelling, his voice trembled when he addressed her:

"I will know!" he said. "I will know what that bracelet said. If you don't tell me I'll find a way——"

He stopped suddenly, and looked over the girl's shoulder at the doorway, his mouth open, his eyes staring, for Talham had brushed aside the agitated Martha Ann, and had stood there, unannounced, for quite a minute.

The girl, following the direction of the old man's eyes, looked round. Her face went pink and white, her hands clasped and unclasped about her crumpled handkerchief.

He came forward with his shoulders bent a little forward, his eyes peering from left to right, a trick of his when he was facing a peril, the extent of which he did not know.

"I thought I heard my name mentioned," he said softly. "I intrude for the second time this day, but I come to take farewell——"

He did not directly address Yvonne, nor did he look at her.

Whatever faults the old man De Costa had, cowardice was not one of them.

"I mentioned your name," he said loudly, "and I am telling you now, Captain Talham, what I have told this young lady: that if you restore that bracelet which you have purloined, I am prepared to take no further action; but otherwise, I shall apply for a warrant for your arrest."

It was, of course, the maddest kind of bluff to put on a man of Talham's calibre.

"Indeed!"

Talham was monstrously polite. The girl's eyes were fixed on him, and her face was a little drawn with anxiety. He smiled at her, an encouraging and an understanding smile.

"We are under the impression," he said regally, "that you have already applied for the warrant, but that the authorities have refused to supply you with the necessary instrument to remove us. As for the bracelet"—he smiled again—"we are prepared, at this moment, to tell you exactly the wording on that extraordinary ornament; but alas! it is in the hands of our excellent friend Tillizinni."

There was an awkward pause. The old man made as if to go.

"You shall hear again from me, Captain Talham," he breathed. "Although I admit the warrant has not been granted, yet in a day or two the necessary affidavits will be received from China."

"We shall be ready to answer any charge you may bring against us," said Talham, "and we would remark that it is no part of our desire to shrink from the ordeal of a public trial. We have supreme and complete faith in the justice of our cause, and we do not shrink from the judgment of our peers."

Evidently De Costa was not anxious to hear the conclusion of the speech. He had long left the room before Talham reached his peroration, which he had so skilfully and adroitly adjusted as to render the presence of the other unnecessary to its dramatic effect.

The girl listened with patience which was beyond praise, though her mind and her heart were in a ferment, and though every moment's delay was torture to her.

As for Mrs. Yale, that wonderful and adaptable woman, she became the sole audience, as far as Talham was concerned. It was she who supplied the murmured applause, who agreed with the deductions he made and the inferences he assumed, though they were tolerably incomprehensible to her. She sat with the proud and happy smile of the well-tested friend who had seen her loyalty vindicated.

At last Talham's address came to an end.

"I want to see you alone," said Yvonne.

There was hardly a break between his last words and her request, so quick she was to take advantage of the silence.

"I have to explain why I wired to you," she said.

Mrs. Yale tiptoed from the room with ostentatious discretion.

"I wired to you," said the girl at last, "because I wanted to see you."

He nodded.

"These people weren't worrying you, were they?" he asked; "because you need not——"

"I know!" she said hastily. "I know! But I'm afraid of what they will do; that they will force me to go out as witness against you. But I will never tell," she said. "Never! never!"

Talham was looking at her in perturbation. It was a new Yvonne Yale he saw; such a one as he had never dreamt of. She took his breath away; he felt himself shaking from head to foot, and at that moment he cursed what he thought was a recurrence of malarial fever. But there was no malarial germ in Talham's veins at that moment. There was something within her that spoke to him, some message which went out in vibrant waves and shook the very centre of life within him.

For the first time in his life, Talham was speechless. He could say nothing; his tongue refused its duty, and Yvonne Yale was in no better case. For her throat had gone dry and husky; it sounded queerly hoarse when she spoke, and she was short of breath, though she had made no recent or unusual exertion.

"Captain Talham," she managed to say, "I wanted to tell you something.... That is why I sent for you. It is a very extraordinary thing I want to say. Suppose they arrest you?"

He shook his head. Even that possibility did not lend him words.

"Suppose they arrest you," she went on in her new, breathless way, with her eyes shining and moist, and her lips parted because of the very physical discomfort of breathing. "Suppose they ask me to go into the witness-box to testify against you... there is a law in England, do you know it—that no— no——"

Again she stopped; the words were so difficult and so impossible.

"There is a law in England," she went on again, "that a wife cannot testify against her husband."

The last words were in a whisper.

For a moment their eyes met. He held them for a breathing space——

CHAPTER 15

SOO WHO CAME BACK

WHEN De Costa went back to his house he was determined at all costs to revenge himself upon the man who had slighted him, and who had brought such misery to his son.

He was prepared to brave any consequences—for an angry man is neither logical nor reasonable, and until his temper cooled he was wilfully blind to the danger which he himself might incur through the publicity of a trial. That was his mood when he reached the gloomy house in Kensington.

Over a frugal dinner he reviewed all the happenings of the past few weeks, and bitterly cursed his luck. Yet the planning and the scheming of years had not altogether ended in nought.

Armed with the information which he was able to give them, his exploration parties would soon be on their way to Mount Li.

The books which were open to Tillizinni were open equally to him. Within a rough radius he also had located the mountain of the Emperor.

His house was in disorder: holland sheets covered most of the furniture, his valuables had been removed to the bank, and his heavy baggage already stood roped and corded for the journey which he had set himself.

He intended travelling across the Trans-Siberian Railway, and sending his trunks on to Shanghai to a trusted agent. The tickets necessary for the journey were in his desk, and his sleeping berth had been booked for some weeks past. This thought made the old man pause: it might be three weeks or a month before he could bring Talham to trial, even supposing that he persuaded the Public Prosecutor to act, and a month was a long time. He decided to sleep on it before taking any further action.

Half-way through dinner, Gregory de Costa paid him an unexpected visit. For two weeks Gregory had seldom been at home except to sleep, and that night, as the old man knew, he had an engagement to dine with a party at a fashionable West End restaurant.

"Hullo!" said the old man, not unkindly. "What has happened to you?"

The young man sank listlessly into a chair by the table.

"I don't know," he said. "I'm just sick of things—that's all!"

"After dining with Soumerez?"

Gregory shook his head. "No," he said, "Soumerez bores me, and I don't feel that I could sit down to dinner at the same table to-night."

There was a little silence, then the young man asked:

"What do you want me to do whilst you're away?"

"Do!" replied his father. "Why, do what you've been doing for the last year or two—just fool around London. I have taken a flat for you in Jermyn Street."

The young man played with a salt-cellar moodily.

"I'd rather go with you," he said.

"That's impossible," said De Costa hurriedly. "I've got to go into a country where all sorts of privations and discomforts have to be encountered, and you're not fit for it. You're a young man, I know," he said gently, "but I've had the life; I have lived in most of these wild places, and my present position is due to the fact. In my young days I undertook certain risks and underwent certain hardships. I have no wish that you should have any of the experiences which were mine as a young man."

Gregory looked at his father curiously.

"I suppose you had a pretty rotten life, didn't you, when you were young?"

Raymond replied with a nod of his head. His son had chosen an appropriate word, for "rotten" indeed was the life De Costa had lived.

There was not an unsavoury transaction in the Philippines or in the far-away trading-places of Asia with which he had not been associated. He had financed more purely illegal schemes, had been behind more piratical expeditions, and had been associated with more heartless villainy than any other of his kind.

Not even the bad old traders of the South Sea Islands could show such a record as his, and even the sanctified odour of Kensington had not altogether dispersed the sinister atmosphere of his early days.

"It is quite impossible for you to come," he went on. "There are all sorts of dangers to be encountered. This is my last expedition."

The young man reached out and took a few grapes from the silver centre-piece, and ate them thoughtfully.

"I am very fond of you," he said suddenly.

The old man did not conceal his pleasure.

"I think," he said softly, "that that is a mutual fondness."

The boy rose after a while and looked at his watch.

"I suppose I had better go along and invent some lie," he said. "Anyway, the dinner will be nearly finished, and I shall be in time for whatever fun there is going after."

His father accompanied him to the door, and watched the disappearing tail-light of the taxi; then he returned to his study.

He spent an hour poring over the translation of the document which was now in Tillizinni's hands. Had he but the jade bracelet, how easy might it be; but he had enough to work on.

Some of the references puzzled him. What were the "spirit steps," for instance; and what of these gigantic cross-bows which were to discharge titanic arrows at the intruder? Possibly two thousand years of rust and decay would have robbed them of their potency.

He picked up some newspaper cuttings dealing with Soo, and smiled, as again and again he came across the phrase which spoke of the "bottling up" of the fugitive. Very well; had these clever English policemen bottled up a man who was now in America, he thought.

He tidied away his documents, and was slipping a rubber band around one little dossier when he stopped, and raised his head, listening.

It was the faintest sound, a tiny, hushed, buzz from one corner of the room.

Now there was only one noise like this in the world that he knew. It was the sound of the secret buzzer which he had had installed communicating with a tiny push near the area door. It had been specially put in to allow his confederates to signal their presence when his servants were out, as they invariably were when visitors of this kind arrived.

Who could it be? He took from his desk a revolver, and made his way noiselessly downstairs to the little hallway which led from the area to the servants' domain.

He crept to the door and listened; there was no sound. The bolts were always kept well oiled. He slipped them back noiselessly and opened the door. Two men were standing there—two small men who made no sound.

"Come in!" he said; but still they made no sign. Then he knew that they were Chinese.

"Come in!" he said again, addressing them in their own language.

He waited until they had closed the door behind, and turning on the electric switch, he flooded the passage with light.

"You!" he gasped.

Well might he be surprised, for these were the two agents of his whom he thought were on their way to China, the men who called themselves "Happy Child" and "Hope of Spring"—who were wanted by the police for the murder of the Chinese Ambassador, and greatly wanted by Soo T'si, for the treacherous slaughter of their comrade—his brother.

"Why do you come here?" he asked angrily.

He spoke in the hissing Canton dialect.

They shuffled uneasily, and the smaller of the two asked sullenly: "Where were we to go, master? Though we escaped the English police, yet Soo T'si has set his society against us, and we have been turned from one refuge to another."

"Why didn't you leave the country?"

"Lord, it was impossible," said the other. "There were men watching boats and trains; we were warned."

"You can't stay here!" said De Costa.

They offered no alternative suggestion, and he led the way upstairs to his room. There they sat on the edge of the two chairs, forlorn, miserable, with that peculiar hunted, haggard look which criminals of all classes assume from necessity.

"Soo is in America now," said De Costa. "If he could get away, why shouldn't you?"

"Master, we were warned," said the taller man again. "A servant from the boat told Hophee," he gave the small man his nickname, "that they were looking for us."

De Costa's mind worked quickly; he had been in some peculiarly dangerous situations before. He must get these men away as quickly as possible.

"You want some money, I suppose," he said, and the smaller man, who seemed to be the ruling spirit, answered monosyllably.

De Costa turned out his pockets and gave him a handful of silver and gold.

"Come to-morrow night," he said, "at the same hour, and I will let you know exactly what plans I have made for you. Is there any danger until to-morrow?"

The small man shook his head.

"You will find your way out, you know the way," said De Costa. "I will come down later and bolt the door after you."

Noiselessly the two men left the room, and De Costa sat at his desk in no enviable mood. He thought he heard the two men speaking together as they went down the stairs to the basement. In his state of tension he imagined that one had called to him sharply, and he opened the door and stepped out into the hall.

"Did you speak?" he asked, and a voice from the basement answered briefly, "No."

He had waited to hear the door open, but realised that so perfectly had it been prepared for midnight visitors that no sound would reach him, and he returned to his desk again.

These men must be got rid of at all hazards; he wondered how. Perhaps now that the attention had been directed towards Soo they might be smuggled out of the country. They had escaped Soo, that was something, for Soo would make short work of them if he knew how grossly he had been betrayed.

The translation of the stolen document still lay on his desk before him, and he folded it up carefully.

"This, at any rate, is something," he said aloud.

"But not all," answered a quiet voice.

He looked up startled.

Before him, in the centre of the room, with his arms folded so that his hands were concealed in his sleeves, stood Soo T'si, and there was a smile upon his face which was not pleasant to see.

"Don't touch your revolver," he said, "for I can shoot you through my sleeve with the greatest of ease."

"I thought you were in America," stammered De Costa.

"I suppose you did," said the other.

He spoke easily in English, a fact which he evidently thought called for some comment.

"I have been speaking nothing but Chinese for the last week or two," he said, "and I was afraid of my English getting stale. Do you mind if I practise it on you?"

He was so affable, and so friendly, that De Costa lost some of his misapprehension.

"I am glad to see you," he said. "I was afraid you had got into serious trouble."

Soo shook his head.

"No, indeed," he said lightly, "one never gets into serious trouble; I got into a particularly foul canal, which compares very favourably with some of the streams of my native land."

He did not attempt to sit down; he did not even move from where he stood, or change his attitude.

"What are your plans?" asked De Costa. "I suppose you know that the police are searching for you?"

Soo nodded.

"I have reason to believe that they are," he said sardonically.

"Can I be of any assistance to you?" asked De Costa.

Soo shook his head.

"I'm afraid that you are absolutely useless to me," he said quietly. "What is that interesting document you have there?"

De Costa would have snatched up the translation from the table, but there was a cold menace in the Chinaman's eye which prevented him.

"It's a little thing," he said vaguely.

"So I see," replied the other. "Turn it round so that I can read it, please."

Like a man fascinated, De Costa obeyed, and Soo took a step nearer the table. He read the sheet through carefully, without moving his hands from the inside of his sleeves, and De Costa wondered why, until he remembered that Soo had threatened him with a concealed pistol.

"You don't seem to trust me." De Costa put a note of reproach into his voice.

"I have very good reasons for not trusting you, De Costa. The last time I was here you swore to me that you had not seen this document, that you had no idea as to where it was. I have discovered since," he went on meditatively, "that you had it all the time, and that you were directly responsible for the treachery of my men, and indirectly for the death of my brother; you told your servants to bring the paper to you at any cost—my brother's life paid for that order."

His voice was even and colourless, and he spoke like a man who was reciting a lesson.

"You are wrong—you are wrong," protested De Costa violently. "I know nothing whatever about it. This paper only came to me a few days ago. I tried to find you——"

Soo shook his head.

"Why do you lie?" he said. "To me, who come from the land of liars, and am skilled in their detection. I know, because the two men you employed, and whom I have been tracking for the last three weeks, have confessed."

"Confessed!" gasped De Costa.

Soo nodded slowly.

"But they have just left," stammered the other.

"They have not left," said Soo quietly, and withdrew his hands from the veiling sleeves.

De Costa went as white as death, for the hands of Soo T'si were scarlet with blood....

* * * *

Twenty minutes later a constable slowly patrolling his beat came to the front of the house De Costa occupied, and automatically threw the light of his lamp over the front door. It seemed in order, and he passed on. He had not gone a dozen yards when he heard a sharp crack, and turned to see a tongue of fire leap from the window of the house he had passed, for even as he had stood watching it, the flames were eating their way through the wooden shutters which covered the window, and the body of old De Costa lay wrapped in a fiery sheet.

CHAPTER 16

IN THE CITY OF HOO-SIN

THE landscape which the travellers beheld was an especially uninviting one; the country was flat, except about the horizon, where a range of low hills were half veiled in mist.

Dreary paddy fields stretched left and right, and the roadway that led down into the village from the slope on which they stood was little more than an uneven track.

"That is our objective," said one of the horsemen.

He looked around for the escort and the mule caravan which was following leisurely behind. There was no sign of either. Five *li* back there was a particularly difficult piece of road to negotiate, and he gathered that with true Chinese philosophy and imperturbability, the muleteers were waiting for the rain to stop.

"That is the village of Cha-k'eo," said the taller of the men.

They were both dressed in the conventional costume of China—thick felt shoes and white stockings, wadded silk coats and padded skirts. On the breast of one was embroidered a fantastic pheasant, and on the top of his little cap he wore a sky-blue button.

That same button had carried them through many seemingly impossible situations.

"It will be raining again in a minute," said Talham with a glance at the sky. "Let us see what Cha-k'eo offers in the way of accommodation."

He cantered down the slope, his sure-footed pony making light of the natural obstacles in the path, and trotted through the one grimy street of the grimy village, ankle deep in black mud.

He drew rein before a dwelling which might have been, in a western clime, a respectable cattle shed. There were two big windows, one of which was half filled up with loose flat bricks, and the other denude of any covering. The door gave entrance to the uninviting interior, but before he could reach the door the proprietor came out.

"How far are we from Shan Shi?" demanded Talham.

"Lord, you are fifty *li*," said the man with a profound bow. "I would advise your excellencies to stay here for the night, for the road is very difficult, and is, moreover, patrolled by bad characters."

He glanced nervously up at Talham as he spoke, for, for all he knew, this might be one of those bad characters against whom he felt it his duty to warn the unwary.

"The advice of the 'chink' in his native habitation," orated Talham as he dismounted slowly, "is liable to be self-interested. On this occasion, however, I think his natural desire to rob us of our cash runs hand in hand with a proper appreciation of real danger."

He spoke in English, and then turned to the fawning landlord.

"My friend," he said benevolently, "tell me the name of the men who patrol this road."

The landlord hesitated. He was evidently afraid to speak openly, yet the authority of Talham's tone, the undeniable rank which he held, and, moreover, the familiarity of the stranger with the dialect of the district, compelled confidence.

"It is the honourable Society of the Bannermen of Heaven," he said humbly. "As your Excellency knows, the city of Taupan, one hundred *lis* south, is having much trouble. There is a rebellion, and His Excellency the Governor has been killed. It is said, too, that his honourable son has returned from the land of the foreign devils."

Talham interrupted him sharply.

"You shall not say," he said, "Iang kuei-tsi, but Iang-ren, for I am a foreigner, and your speech is offensive to me."

The man bowed low. He was frightened almost to death, and was shaking in every limb, for the stories of the foreigner, and the events which had followed the taking of Pekin, had been exaggerated up and down the country. Moreover, as he knew, Iang-ren filled the Chinese army, holding high positions, as this great one evidently did.

"Lord, it was a slip of my tongue," he said naïvely, "as we used to speak of foreigners in the days of Ihoch'uan."

He gave the Boxers their full title, and Talham nodded.

"Take the horses and let them be cleaned and fed," he said. "My friend and I desire your best room."

The man led the way with many apologies into the interior of his shed. To Talham's surprise, there was an interior room which had few of the objectionable features which Chinese caravanserai frequently present. It was tolerably clean, and free from the disagreeable odour of opium smoke.

A long, low *kang* occupied the full length of one wall, and when an hour later the mule train came up, and rugs were spread upon the Chinese equivalent for bedstead, and a brazier of burning charcoal was brought in, the travellers had good reason for congratulating themselves upon the comfort of their lodging.

That the arrival of foreigners in a tiny village would attract the entire population goes without saying, but a word from Talham dismissed the rabble, and the landlord was placed outside the door with two of the escort to see that the foreign "lords" were not disturbed.

"You may say," said Talham, "that we have now reached the most critical portion of our journey."

Tillizinni was examining a map by the light of a Chinese lamp.

"If your surmises are right," he said, "the Mount Li described in the Second Emperor's account, is that somewhat insignificant hill that we saw as we came over the rise to the village."

Talham nodded.

"I am satisfied that it is," he said.

He seemed less inclined to orate than Tillizinni had ever remembered him. Indeed, so marked was his depression that presently the detective referred to it.

"I know," said the other uncomfortably; "but the fact is, I am not too satisfied with the progress we have made, and less satisfied——did you hear what he said?"

He jerked his head in the direction of the landlord.

"I did," said Tillizinni. "But, fortunately, my knowledge of the dialect isn't as good as yours. I find that a conversance with 'Mandarin Chinese' isn't always as useful as it might be."

"He said that there had been a revolt in Taupan," said Talham, "and that His Excellency the Governor had been killed, and that his son occupied what amounted to the kingship of this district. Do you realise who that man is?"

"Not Soo?" asked the detective.

Talham nodded.

"That's just who it is," he said, "and he has tricked us." He was silent for a moment, then, "Anyway, I'm glad he's here," he said. "I've been getting jumpy about Yvonne."

The thought that Soo might be within six or seven days' journey had troubled him.

"It is better he should be here than there."

He was almost cheerful at the thought.

"He'll hear to-morrow that we're in the district," he went on, "and then the fun is going to begin."

Before he went to sleep that night, Tillizinni saw that his revolver was loaded, and placed it under his pillow within reach of his hand. News travels fast in a country which does not depend so much upon the up-to-date telegraph, as upon some mysterious means of communication which is peculiarly the secret of a semi-barbarian people.

They were not to be disturbed that night, however, and Tillizinni woke to find the day broken and rain still falling heavily. Breakfast was prepared by the servant whom Talham had engaged at Shanghai, but in spite of the wretched surroundings and the unpleasant prophecy of the day, the two men made a good meal.

"Our immediate danger," said Talham, "lies in the fact that we are going straight to Hoo Sin, a city which is in some way allied to our friend's stronghold. What makes it rather awkward is the fact that Hoo Sin must be our base for a week or two, or, at any rate, until we can locate the tomb."

Tillizinni nodded.

"I know the mandarin personally," Talham went on. "An Oriental of exceeding affability, and it would seem to me that the possibility of the Oriental mind——"

He might have developed his speech into a discourse on Chinese metaphysics, but Tillizinni interrupted him.

"We have to go," he said, "and the roads are pretty bad."

They were worse than the men anticipated, and the progress along the wild and tortuous path, which was dignified by the name of road, was a painful experience.

The two leaders of the expedition could not afford to leave their escort. They were in an enemy's country, and although the fifty soldiers which the First Mandarin of the Empire had supplied them was a formidable body, Talham knew the Chinamen well enough to know that they could not be depended upon if they were convinced that the object of his trip was the desecration of a grave.

He would gain nothing by explaining to them that he had no intention of robbing the grave of its treasures, or that he sought some wonderful mechanical secret which the dead years held—that was too supple a distinction for words.

He had sent messengers ahead a week before to collect as many of the soldiers who had served in his regiment as could be found, to meet him at Hoo Sin. Soo might send a story flaming through the bazaar that would set the city of Hoo Sin in a ferment—if he dared. That reservation was Talham's only hope.

If Soo himself had designs upon the tomb, desired exact knowledge as to its location, and wished for himself to unravel the mystery and to take the treasures of the dead king, he would be silent. Once he set the city in a ferment he might spoil whatever chance Talham had of achieving his object, but he would just as assuredly defeat his own ends, and might, moreover, call down upon the city of Hoo Sin a detachment of Imperial troops, to say nothing of commissions of enquiry.

The thought comforted Talham as he jogged along, the rain falling in sheets above his head, the pony under him stumbling across rocks and through pools of liquid mud, towards the blurred horizon.

There is no more cheerless sight in the world than a Chinese landscape; on either side the flat black land stretched drearily to the stunted hills.

Now and again they would pass a half-ruined temple or a collection of squalid huts, too tiny it seemed to bear the long name which custom had given to them.

Night was falling when they clattered up the broad irregular street, littered with garbage, and passed through the high, gaunt city gates of Hoo Sin.

The rain had ceased, and the city was filled with people who looked curiously at the "foreign devils," whom no Chinese costume could disguise. No demonstration was made, however, as the two men and their escort rode up to the Yamen and dismounted.

There was the inevitable delay.

The Mandarin's assistant who interviewed him in the courtyard of the Yamen at Talham's request for an interview had disappeared. He returned in a few minutes full of apologies and regrets. His Excellent Lio-le was indisposed, and regretted that he was unable to see the honourable visitors.

Talham turned to Tillizinni and said in English: "That is pretty ominous. If old Lio-le won't see us, it is because he is afraid of our friend Soo."

"Is it necessary that we should see him?" asked Tillizinni.

Talham nodded. He turned again to the secretary.

"You will go at once to His Excellency and say a Mandarin of the Empire, and a bearer of the Imperial Banner, desires an immediate audience in the name of the Daughter of Heaven, the Dowager Empress."

The man bowed low and went back to the Yamen.

He returned almost immediately with the request that the two should follow him.

They passed through the big, cold entrance-hall into the throne-room of the Yamen. As they entered, a man, sitting in solitary state at one end of the room, fanning himself mechanically, rose and shuffled forward, stopping within a few paces of his visitors to give the customary Chinese kow-tow.

The old Mandarin was stout and ordinarily jovial, but now his face wore a troubled and fretful expression.

"Why do you come to this city?" he asked with asperity. "Where do you come from? How many miles have you travelled by road?" and so through the whole gamut of questions which are conventionally asked by those in authority of those who come within their sphere.

The servants brought tea—little cups and placed them handy. Tillizinni, to whom a cup of tea would have been very refreshing at that moment, almost mechanically stretched out his hand to take one, when Talham stopped him.

"To take tea," he said, "is a sign that the interview is finished, and I have much to ask our friend before the tea-drinking stage arrives."

"Does the honourable stranger intend staying in our perfectly beastly little village for any time?" asked the Mandarin.

Talham bowed.

"Though we are unworthy to walk through the beautiful streets of this most divine city," he said, "we wish your noble citizens to tolerate our disagreeable presence for the space of a moon."

The Mandarin eyed him coldly.

"At this season of the year," he said significantly, "my mean and despicable city is very unhealthy for the honourable foreigner."

"Yet we will stay," answered Talham promptly, "if your Excellency will afford protection to two insignificant animals who, by the fortune of the gods, are very precious to the Daughter of Heaven, the Dowager Empress. So much does the Daughter of Heaven regard us," he continued, "that though we are as dirt under her feet, every moon there will come a courier from Pekin to your glorious community to seek information as to our welfare, and if"—he was apologetic—"if we are so base and horrible that we cannot find health in so salubrious a spot, the courier will return to the Daughter of Heaven with news of our misfortune."

It was threat for threat, and Talham carried the heavier guns. His passport was in order, and he was commended by the highest in the land, and at the end ran the "tremble and obey" of an exalted Prince of the Royal House.

CHAPTER 17

THE TOMB LOCATED

THE Mandarin's face was a study. Between fear of consequence, the sure reprisal which would come to him from the Government if his visitors were harmed, and the fear of the greater and more immediate danger from a cause unknown to the visitors, but very accurately guessed, he was in a very painful quandary.

"If the honourable strangers will accept the hospitality of my miserable pigsty," he said sullenly, "for a few days, at least, I will ensure them safety from the disorderly characters who populate my unsavoury town."

He reached out for the cup, and the two men followed suit, for they were dismissed.

They made their way to the house to whither Talham had already directed his muleteers. The two men rode back through the bazaar by themselves. There was nothing in the attitude of the people to suggest that they had organised opposition to fear. The scowls and half-muttered implications which greeted them was the usual lot of the Western traveller in that part of the world.

Talham's keen eyes surveyed the crowd as the horses made their way slowly through the street leading to the western end of the city. He was looking for a familiar face, and presently he found it. Over the heads of the throng he saw a man standing quietly with his back to the entrance of a fruit shop.

Talham tilted his chin ever so slightly, and the man, though seemingly unobservant of his action, repeated the motion.

So far so good. Some of his men were in the city. He had never depended upon the escort. He knew that they would fly at the first hint of danger.

But they were armed with modern weapons, and since it was necessary for his purpose that the various members of his old regiment should be effectively equipped, what easier way of bringing arms into this territory than in the hands of Imperial troops?

He had this in his mind when they reached the little caravanserai which was to be the headquarters of the expedition.

It was a one-roofed dwelling set in the middle of a yard and surrounded by a high wall. The building proper was divided into two parts, the smaller of which Talham directed to be cleaned out (for it was indescribably filthy) and prepared for the lodging of himself and his friend.

He handed the other to the captain of the escort.

It seemed to Tillizinni hardly large enough to accommodate forty men, but then Tillizinni was not so well acquainted with the habits and customs of the Chinese soldiery as was his companion.

"It would take a hundred and forty," was the cool reply when Tillizinni cast doubt upon its capacity.

They made the little room—it was no more than a stable from their point of view—as comfortable as possible, spreading a carpet unpacked from one of the mules and fixing up a little much-needed ventilation.

The walls were thick, and an inspection of the outer wall which surrounded the courtyard was satisfactory. The place could withhold a siege given a few improvements, and these improvements Talham set himself out to make without further delay.

He sent into the town for workmen, and as soon as day broke he had them knocking out bricks from the wall at regular intervals.

Some news of this must have come to the Mandarin, for he sent a hurried message demanding Talham's presence.

The tall man rode out along to the Yamen and saw his unwilling host.

"News has come to me," said the Mandarin without preliminary, "that your honourable self and your honourable friend are engaged in making alterations to the outer wall of the King-Li. Now, such conduct," he wagged his finger at Talham, "is against my faith. I cannot save-face if it is known that my protection is so unworthy to the honourable foreigners that he must fortify himself against the citizens of this town."

"Lao-ae," said Talham earnestly, and he employed his full knowledge of Mandarin Chinese to further his eloquence, "though I am but as the mud under the wheels of your cart, though I am not fitted even to prostrate myself in your presence, yet the Daughter of Heaven thinks so well of me that it would not please me if I caused the great and beautiful lady sorrow by my death. Moreover," he added, "my love and esteem for you, who are known from one end of the Empire to the other as a just and wise ruler, and one marked out for special promotion to the Governorship of Shu Shung——"

A little gleam came into the Mandarin's eye at this broad hint, though he might have known that Talham could lie as well as any other man.

"Yet," the big man went on, "because I have this affection for you, I am terrified lest trouble come upon your nobility through some mischance to my miserable carcase."

The Mandarin was silent.

The reference to a governorship, the dreams of his life, set him thinking. Presently he said mildly:

"I have talked with your Excellency, and my duty is finished—*puh p'a!* You have nothing to fear."

With that he allowed Talham to return to his work of putting the inn into a condition of defence.

Talham had posted two sentries at the gate, and people were only allowed in two at a time.

That there should be a big crowd before the foreigner's quarters—a crowd of curious, peering, tip-toeing, interested Celestials, goes without saying, for the Chinese are tremendously curious.

Every now and again the officer of the guard would come to Talham, busy with Tillizinni, working out calculations as to distances and depths, with the information that a stranger wished to see him. Talham would walk patiently to the gate, exchange a few words with the man who desired an audience, and, at a nod, the stranger would be allowed to pass.

By the evening of the first day there were occupying the little compound some forty soldiers and some forty-five nondescript Chinamen who had turned up from nowhere in particular, and Talham's estimate as to the sleeping capacity of the improvised barrack-room proved to be no exaggeration.

He had made one wise provision, and that was that the arms of the escort, including even the sword and revolver of the officer commanding when he was not on duty, should be stacked in a smaller room. In addition, he had all the ammunition which he had brought with him similarly stored. It cramped the small apartment considerably and filled up every available piece of space, but Talham was insistent upon this, though the officer demurred.

In the morning, when the new guard mounted, they took over the rifles of the men who had been on duty on the previous day.

On the third day Talham went out to make an inspection of the problematic Mount Li. He left before daybreak and only halted at the city gates because they were not open at that hour.

He did not return until near sunset, and when he did he was immensely hungry, not having, as he said, eaten since he set forth, save a couple of dubious eggs which he secured at a village en route.

"I am satisfied we are on the right track," he said, "and I am more satisfied because a farmer in the neighbourhood tells me that some men have been over from Tai-San quite recently exploring the mountain.

"It isn't a mountain really," he went on. "As a matter of fact I have a theory that previous to the Emperor's death, it had no existence at all."

He described the place.

It lay in the neck or dip of two hills, and, apparently, had been filled up so that the top of the hill should offer an unbroken sky-line to the traveller in the valley beneath.

"There is no doubt at all in my mind," said Talham emphatically, "that this is the tomb. We have now to find the guarded entrance. You can see the slope of the hills before they were earthed up quite distinctly, and I think I have found the ruins of an old temple half buried near the crest of one of these."

He read again the Second Emperor's description.

"That's it," he said. "He caused trees and grass to be planted so that it might appear a part of the mountain."

"But why should he have been brought so far away from the capital?" asked Tillizinni.

"That is a question which we have never satisfactorily settled. You might as well ask," said the other, "why the Ming Emperors wanted huge stone elephants to indicate the way to their tombs. There is no reason for anything in China, except that if you see a thing for which there is absolutely no excuse, you may be satisfied that that *is* the excuse!"

"You are almost lucid," said Tillizinni with a smile.

He himself was enjoying the trip immensely; he found the relaxation which he needed so badly. There was no telephone; nobody brought him tangles of mystery to unravel. He was living amidst actualities, amongst primitive forces, in a land where murder was a commonplace everyday incident, and where the murderers seldom troubled to hide their tracks. He recognised that there was considerable danger to himself and to his companion if the real object of the visit was ever discovered.

Soo would be very active just now; his spies would long since have carried news of the arrival of the "foreign devils."

It needed no spy, as it happened, for the Mandarin himself, with a keen desire to "save-face" all round, had sent a private courier with many apologies to his powerful rival, and Soo's agents were active.

The first indication of trouble that Talham had seen, took the shape of a jagged stone which was thrown at him as he passed through the bazaar on an afternoon on his return from one of his expeditions.

That evening he found the soldiers sullen, and he was interviewed by the officer of the guard.

"My insignificant men," said the officer, "have petitioned me, asking that your Noble Beneficence will restore to them their arms, because they feel afraid and ashamed also, since the common people of the bazaar laugh at them."

"You may tell your men to go to the devil," said Talham without finesse.

But an hour later the officer had returned, this time with a fresh grievance.

"My men," he said boldly, "do not like these strangers sleeping in the same room with them, for they come from another province, and are members of another society."

"Captain," said Talham patiently, "if you come to me again with such stories, I will have you beaten on the feet."

Later, he was to receive private advice from one of these same strangers, that the men had had a meeting and were discussing the advisability of leaving the compound in a body.

This threat took definite shape the next morning, when the officer came yet again in some fear to announce the intention of his men.

"These pigs," he said humbly, "will leave your Excellency unless their arms are returned."

"Tell them they may leave," said Talham cheerfully, "and they will get no arms from me."

The situation outside the gates was even more serious. A rumour had broken through the bazaar that the foreigners had come to mark out the land for a railway.

The people in this province were fanatics on the question of "fire-horses," and every hour the feeling grew against the intruders.

Talham suspected the Mandarin of fostering this feeling. Twice when he had called at the Yamen His Excellency had been indisposed and only his "men-shang" was visible. On the occasion of the second visit (he had called in on his way back from one of his trips of exploration) a hostile crowd surrounded his horse, and somebody from the outskirts of the crowd had thrown a stone which narrowly missed his face.

Instantly the big man turned his horse, scattering the people left and right. He had seen the face of the thrower, and reaching down he caught him by the collar of his jacket and galloped with him at full speed through the streets, his prisoner alternately running and stumbling in the powerful grip of his captor.

Talham reached the compound and the gates closed behind him; then he turned his attention to his captive.

"Seize that man," he said in Chinese, and the guard obeyed the order reluctantly.

Talham dismounted and came to where the man stood.

"Why did you throw stones?" he asked.

"Because you are a 'foreign devil' and are going to bring the 'fire-horses' across the graves of our ancestors," said the Chinaman.

"Who told you this?"

"Everybody knows it," answered the prisoner, emboldened by the fact that he had escaped immediate punishment.

"You are not of this town. Where do you come from?"

The man hesitated.

"I come from Tang Ti," he said suddenly.

"Oh, liar, and son of a liar!" said Talham. "You come from Tai-pau."

The man shifted uneasily on his feet.

"Who sent you?" asked Talham. "Let me see his shoulder."

Again the guard showed some reluctance to obey, and Talham himself stepped forward and tore the blouse of the man from his neck and scrutinised the yellow flesh for the sign of the tell-tale tattoo.

It was there.

"Go back to Lao-ae Soo T'si," he said, "and tell him that I know who is at the bottom of all this hostility. I speak to you fairly," he added, "because I see you are a student, and perhaps you are the son of great parents."

The young man nodded.

"I am the son of a son of a Mandarin," he said with pride.

Your Chinaman will never deny his parentage if it be sufficiently illustrious.

"Well, then, son of a son of a Mandarin, or son of a son of a gun, whichever you are," said Talham, "go quickly from this place and take with you as many of your friends as you can find."

With that he turned the man loose.

That night Talham's escort deserted in a body, and the big man was jubilant.

"It couldn't have happened better," he said. "I was wondering how I could get rid of the beggars."

Instantly he assembled his own men and armed them. He was satisfied of their loyalty, and distributed ammunition that same night. For some reason the hostility in the bazaar had ceased after that one act of stone-throwing. The escort disappeared from the town as if by magic.

It was not a healthy sign as Talham knew, because armed or disarmed, they were men who carried the Imperial badge upon their breast, and their hurried departure was ominous.

He rode out now to Mount Li with an escort of four of his own men. He thought he had detected the entrance to the tomb.

Half-way down the hill two straight ledges of the rock jutted out. They ran parallel to one another for about twenty yards, and then curved downward into the earth. From a distance they had every appearance of being placed there by nature, but something induced Talham to take a closer view. He made the ascent over the loose rubble and through the stunted bushes which covered the hillside.

He examined them carefully, and in the end he had no doubt whatever that they were placed there by the hand of man.

This would be the entrance, if entrance there were.

He had looked for an opening to the tomb at the foot of the hill. Apparently, it was half-way up that he must seek it.

"I am perfectly sure," he told Tillizinni that night, "that if we can dig between those two pieces of sculpture, for pieces of sculpture they are, ingeniously carved to represent natural rock, and at the same time to afford some interested person a clue as to the whereabouts of the hill, we shall come upon the famous bronze door which hides the secret of the Emperor's artificers.

"We shall have to do our digging by night," he went on; "but I don't anticipate digging very far. From what I have seen of the entrance to the tomb, it looks as though a few more showers of rain would wash the bronze door into view."

Preparations were far advanced towards the final examination of the hill, and it was in the afternoon previous to the day on which the attempt was to be made, that a courier came hot-foot from the Yamen summoning Talham to the Mandarin's presence.

He had not seen the great man for some days, and wondering what was new, and somewhat apprehensive, since it was quite on the cards that Pekin may have sent an Imperial edict prohibiting any further research, he hurried to the Yamen, and was instantly admitted to the presence of the Mandarin, who received him with great geniality.

"A courier has brought a letter for your honourable self from Pekin," and he picked it up from a little ebony table.

The letter, whatever it was, was enclosed in a large envelope covered with Chinese characters.

Talham opened the outer envelope slowly, dreading the contents. They proved to be two letters, and the first of these was startling enough, for it was addressed to Miss Yvonne Yale, c/o the British Consul, Hoo Sin.

Talham stared. There was no British Consul in Hoo Sin.

With a start he recognised the handwriting as that of Mrs. Yale.

The second was addressed to himself, and was from the same lady. He tore it open quickly and read its contents with a sinking heart. It ran:

"Dear Captain Talham,—

"Yvonne left London yesterday for China to join you. She is travelling by the overland route.

"Naturally, I felt very chary of allowing her to go by herself, but your telegram was so emphatic that I could not deny the dear girl the pleasure which I know she will feel in meeting you.

"I am sure you will telegraph her arrival the moment she gets to Hoo Sin, and that the ladies who have so kindly offered her their hospitality will not be disappointed in my gem! I should be glad if you will thank them for me."

"My God!" muttered Talham, for he had sent no cablegram to the girl or to her mother.

CHAPTER 18

IN THE CAVERN OF THE DEAD

"The honourable stranger has received bad news," said the Mandarin.

Talham looked at him thoughtfully. Could he help?

"I have received very bad news," he said, "with which I will not assail your magnificent ear. Yet I would ask you this. Where is the nearest telegraph town?"

The Mandarin considered.

"There is one at Tai Pan," he said, looking straightly at the other. "That is the nearest. Otherwise you would have to go to Cho Sin, which is a hundred and fifty *li* from here."

"I shall send to Tai Pan," said Talham, and took his leave with a little ceremony.

All messages that went through Tai Pan would, of course, be seen by Soo. It was Cho Sin or nothing.

He got back to the compound, and found Tillizinni making an inspection of the walls.

"I've bad news," he said, and with remarkable brevity told the contents of the letter.

"The girl has been lured here by Soo," said Tillizinni; "that's evident."

"My God, she may be in Tai Pan now!" said Talham.

"He would have met her at one of the wayside stations on the Trans-Siberian. It's horrible, Tillizinni, horrible!"

Tillizinni considered.

"One thing is evident," he said after a while. "Once you have penetrated the tomb of the Emperor you must clear out quick. Why not make the attempt to-night and leave China by way of Tai Pan? You have fifty men. Make a dash upon Soo's stronghold and take your chance of finding Yvonne there."

Talham thought for awhile.

"That is one scheme," he said; "but I think I know a better. I will leave twenty men to defend this place and use this as my base. We'll go to the tomb to-night."

Talham could have let the tomb go—but there was nothing to be gained by this. Mount Li was on the way to Tai Pan—the two expeditions could be accomplished in one night. He could reach Tai Pan before the dawn.

Soo would not be prepared for an early morning rush upon his city.

Prudence and interest dictated parallel courses.

Talham had committed to memory the instructions which the dead builders had left, some of which apparently conflicted with those upon the jade bracelet.

He had written down the words engraved upon the bracelet, and now he read them again.

"I am Shun, the son of the great mechanic, Shoo Shun, upon whom the door fell when the Emperor passed. This my father told me before the day, fearing the treachery of the Eunuchs.

"Behold the pelican on the left wall with the bronze neck. Afterwards the spirit steps, afterwards rivers of silver, afterwards door of bronze. Here Emperor... behind a great room filled with most precious treasures."

"I guess he's a little wrong in the bronze door part of it," said Tillizinni. "It's possible that there were two sets of disloyal mechanics planning to secure the Emperor's treasure, and made provisions for entering and retiring at the proper moment."

That afternoon his men left singly and in two's and three's, making for the rendezvous, and when night fell, Tillizinni and Talham, both men heavily armed, rode out into the dark streets, and the door of the compound closed behind them.

They had left twenty-three men under a trusted old officer who had been with Talham in the Northern wars, and the remainder of the party were picked up beyond the city walls.

They rode along the mud track which led to Mount Li.

It was eleven o'clock before they debouched from the road and picked a way across the rough, uncultivated land which sloped up to the Emperor's tomb.

The party dismounted at the foot of the hill and took shelter in a little gully, and six men only accompanied the two Europeans in their climb. These carried spades and picks, a spare one each for Talham and Tillizinni, and the eight men attacked the soft earth with feverish haste.

It was easier work than even Talham had anticipated, and after an hour's work Tillizinni's spade struck something hard and metalled.

"It's the door," he said exultantly.

He cleared away a space and examined his find with the aid of a pocket lamp.

Here the hill fell sheerly, and it was at the foot of a sharp slope that the top of the door was discovered.

Although the hill fell steeply there seemed to be no place from whence a door might slide down in its grooves to block the entrance of the cave.

This was the only doubt that had been in Talham's mind, but the explanation suddenly occurred to him.

"I see now," he said excitedly. "It opens inward on hinges at the top."

This probably was the case.

They continued digging for half an hour before they reached the foot of the bronze door.

Contrary to his expectations, there was no engraving upon the panel. It was of solid bronze, green with age.

The men scraped carefully away at its foot, and then Talham on one side and Tillizinni on the other, groped for the image between the two stones. It was a long time before Talham discovered his, but Tillizinni's was soon revealed. It had deteriorated until it was little more than the thickness of a curtain ring.

Tillizinni looked at it closely. It had been shaped crudely by these old dishonest artisans, and even now its extemporised character was revealed in the imperfection of the circle.

"Got it!" he heard Talham grunt.

"Does it give at all?"

"Yes," said the other, "but, gently! It is any odds on the connection being rotten with age."

"Now!" said Tillizinni. "Are you ready? Now!"

He put a gentle strain upon the ring, and it gave, ever so little.

He was afraid to put his full strength upon it for fear it broke away in his hand.

"Again," said Talham's voice.

Tillizinni pulled gently. Suddenly, without a warning, there was a horrible squeak, which it seemed could be heard for miles, and the great door sunk as if the earth had swallowed it up, and the big black entrance of the cave was revealed.

From here on, they must depend upon their own exertions. The Chinamen declined civilly enough to assist any further. So far they had acted in accordance with their tenets. Beyond that they might not go.

Talham understood and dismissed them, telling them to wait at the bottom of the hill.

He flashed an electric torch about the entrance of the cave. It was a large spacious place carved out of a solid rock. At intervals around its grim walls were placed huge statues in fantastic shapes, extending from the dim roof to its polished floor.

Talham looked at them without awe.

He felt something about his feet, and flashed the light down. He was treading on a little heap of bones. Further examination revealed a dozen more such pitiful relics of the long-dead artisans who had perished that they might not reveal the secret of the Emperor's tomb.

For two thousand years they had laid thus, through all the centuries pregnant with progress and with world-shaking events; as they had fallen in death so they remained.

Talham was a curious mixture of the sentimental and the practical.

The practical side of him brushed the relics aside with his foot as he walked forward sending the gleam of his light flashing up to the roof.

Yes, there were the two silver lamps; they were black under the tarnish, but the delicacy of the workmanship was apparent.

Reaching up his hand, Talham could just clutch the dangle tassel beneath the first lamp.

"Watch that entrance," he said, and put his lamp upon the black door at the further end of the vault.

He pulled and a chain gave slowly. Then, with a swift rush, the door before him opened in the middle and parted. As it did, from the interior of the inner chamber came a loud crash, something whizzed between the two men, passed through the opening where the bronze door had been, and buried itself in the hillside without.

"Phew!" said Talham, "that crossbow did work after all."

He wiped the sweat from his forehead with the back of his hand.

"I trust nothing else unpleasant happens," he said.

He looked round for the pelican which had been referred to on the bracelet, but could see no sign of any such ornament.

The steps leading down into the inner room were clean and smooth. They were of white marble, save in the centre was what appeared to be a carpet. On closer inspection this proved to be "treads" of jade, two feet wide and exactly in the centre of the stairway.

"Those are the spirit steps," said Talham. "You had better keep to them."

"What are spirit steps?" asked Tillizinni in astonishment.

"It's an old Chinese idea, and you'll find it in a good many temples," replied Talham briefly. "It is popularly supposed to be the steps up and down which the spirits of the departed pass to their devotions, and is never under any circumstances used by mortals."

"For a moment," he said with a facetiousness which seemed to Tillizinni to be entirely out of place, "we will regard ourselves as disembodied and keep to the spirit steps."

He walked down gingerly. Half way to the bottom were two little niches on which stood carved representations of two of the earlier Chinese deities. He stopped and looked at them thoughtfully. Then, leaning over, he lifted one down. It was a tremendous weight, and he staggered under it, but Talham was curious to see the result of his experiment.

He placed the statue upon one of the white marble steps which ran down at either side of him. For a moment nothing happened, and then the stairs opened under it and it disappeared.

In a second came the tinkle of smashing steel.

"I thought so," said Talham. "If we had departed from the spirit steps, we should have fallen into a most unpleasant mess."

He watched the yawning hole where the steps had been. Three had disappeared.

In a few seconds they came slowly back and jarred themselves back into their place.

"They are balanced on an arm below," explained Tillizinni. "I saw something of that sort in Burma years ago."

He led the way down, and so they came to the inner chamber.

"Look!" gasped Talham, and well might he be astonished, for as they put their foot upon the lower stairs the whole of the inner chamber was flooded with soft light.

It came from the cornices in the roof and was reflected down from the glittering blue firmament of an artificial heaven.

"It's electric!" said Talham in a whisper. "I never dreamt of this."

Whilst they stood upon the steps the light continued. When they took a step forward it went out. They returned to the lower step and the room was again illuminated.

"It was from this step, you may be sure, that the Second Emperor took his last view of his father," said Tillizinni. "There is your river."

They looked down in silent wonderment. There at their feet was China—China as it was known to the ancients, with little townships cunningly modelled, and the ever-moving river flowed from hill to sea. So it had been flowing for two thousand years.

"Stand on the step," said Talham, "and let me see."

He stepped down quickly and leant over one of the tiny streams that wandered tortuously through an artificial garden.

"It's quicksilver all right," he said.

At the far end of the room was a great block of polished black stone, and upon this rested a stone coffin. The pedestal was reached by three steps, but the steps were indistinguishable. They were covered with rags, and, as it seemed, little pieces of white, glittering wood.

Talham surveyed them reverently. These, then, were the unfortunate creatures of joy, who had gone down to death with their lord.

He made a rapid survey of the great stone room. At either side he saw a square pit, and flashed a light down upon the white gems that still glittered and sparkled in the light.

He was seeking something else, and presently he found it—a little box of jade, upon the roof of which was the faded remnants of an inscription. More to the point, there had been carved on its side, and was as fresh to-day as when it left the carver's hands, two thousand years before, the words:

"This is the secret of the philosopher."

He lifted the box and put it under his arm and made his way back to Tillizinni.

"We can't leave yet," said the detective, all a-quiver with excitement. He felt he was on the verge of a great discovery. "We must find by what means this room is lighted."

Then he remembered the urgent business that waited in Tai Pan.

"Perhaps we can come back," he said regretfully, for he knew that when they had once passed through the portals they would never again visit the last home of the First Emperor.

Talham led the way upward, and was within twenty feet of the silver door when somebody laughed, and the laugh rang hollowly through the vaulted chamber. He looked up. Before he was conscious of what was happening and before his hand could drop to the pistol at his side, a voice called mockingly:

"You have ample time to complete your investigations, Captain Talham."

It was the voice of Soo, and it came from the head of the stairs.

Talham and Tillizinni whipped out their revolvers and fired together, and again came the laugh and something more ominous—the rumble of a moving door.

They sprang up the stairs together, but before Talham could swing himself through, the door had closed with a clang and a crash. They were trapped in the house of the dead!

CHAPTER 19

THE YAMEN OF T'SI SOO

YVONNE YALE was in the little room which overlooked the courtyard of the Governor's yamen. She sat on the edge of the *kang*, her hands clasped on her knees, her face tense and pale.

So this was the meaning of it—the meaning of that telegram which had sent her flying across Europe into the barbaric regions of Asia, that had set her down at a little wayside station, where a polite and tidy escort waited to convey her to her lover.

With no knowledge of the language, she had hesitated before accompanying them, and had stood on the platform for half an hour before she at last yielded to the agitated entreaties of the officer in charge of the escort—a man with little English, and who knew that his life depended upon his persuading the beautiful Westerner to accompany him.

Why had not Talham come himself to receive her? The officer-escort had been full of apologies and explanations in his pidgin English. Captain Talham was honourably engaged, also he had honourably hurt his foot digging and could not ride.

He had not sent her a line of welcome, which was strange, but she had come so far, and it was absurd to shrink from the thirty miles journey which she was promised.

A luxurious palanquin, borne upon mules and lined with rose silk, was a tempting conveyance. The bottom of the shaky vehicle was covered with down cushions. That novelty of the silken nest pleased her.

An impassive bystander, watching the departure of the caravan, sidled up on some pretext to where she sat and muttered under his breath "Ko'lien," shaking his head the while.

She repeated it, "Ko'lien."

"What does it mean?"

The officer rode by her side and chatted with her in such English as he could master.

It occurred to her, after they had gone some ten *li* on the road, to ask carelessly the meaning of the words which the strange Chinaman had employed.

"Ko'lien," repeated the escort with a beaming smile. "He mean makee piecee solly."

"Makee piecee solly," she repeated. "So it meant 'I am sorry for you!' Why should he be sorry?"

Later she understood, and was sorry enough for herself.

Her destination was farther than thirty miles. They halted that night at a village where rough but reasonable accommodation was provided for her, and Hoo Sin was promised in the morning.

But it was not until the evening of the next day, after hard going, that they passed through the deserted streets of a big city, and turned into a walled courtyard and came to a halt before a handsome building.

She got out of the palanquin, stiff and aching. She was feeling depressed and untidy, and in no mood to meet the man of her choice.

They made it clear to her that she might go to her room, and for this she was grateful.

Again there was no Talham, but the commander of the escort was at pains to explain that possibly her lover would not be in till later, and that he had not expected her arrival so soon.

She was shown to the room which she now occupied, a curious little room filled with Western knick-knacks, and evidently prepared for her. She had made her hurried toilet, and was wondering exactly how she could summon the attendant, when the door opened and a Chinaman walked into the room.

She saw at once that he was of a different class to the men who had escorted her. His garments were of silk and beautifully embroidered; his face was almost aesthetic, his mien lofty and commanding.

"I hope you have everything you want," he said in perfect English.

She gave a gasp of horror, for she recognised the voice of the man in whose power she had been before.

He smiled genially, reading her thoughts.

"Yes," he said, smoothing the breast of his silk jacket delicately. "I am Soo T'si, whom your friends 'bottled up.'"

There was something in that expression which had been particularly hateful to the man. His weakness lay in his vanity, perhaps, and the implied reflection upon his inability to evade the English police had rankled.

"Bottled up," he repeated, as with relish; "and now I think I have you 'bottled up' also."

"You must let me leave here at once," she said.

"I am sorry that cannot be done," he replied coolly. "You see, you are not in Hoo Sin. You are in Tai Pan, which is my particular stronghold, and where I hold certain rights which you would describe as feudal. I owe you an apology," he went on, "for telegraphing to you."

"Then it was you?" she said.

He nodded.

"I thought you would have guessed that. Hoo Sin is some distance," he went on, "and I am afraid your lover is pursuing his warlike preparations in blissful ignorance of the fact that some forty *li* away the lady of his heart is a prisoner in the hands of his worst enemy."

She made no reply.

What use was there in arguing with this man? Whatever was to happen, no word of hers could move him to pity or to compassion. She must face whatever had to be faced with all the courage which God would give her in her extremity.

Fortunately, Soo did not prolong his visit. He made a few enquiries as to whether she was comfortable, and left her, having first brought into the room a Chinese girl who was to act as her servant.

"I have decided what I shall do with you," was his parting speech, "and you may be sure it will be something highly entertaining."

For two long days, where every minute seemed an hour and every hour a year, she was kept prisoner in the little room under the roof of the Yamen. No indignity was offered to her. Her commands, such as did not procure greater freedom of movement, were instantly obeyed. Even her food was cooked in Western style by Soo's own chef.

They called him Ho-Lao-Ae, "the river Mandarin," and the name of Soo T'si seemed to be unknown to them. That he was a person of the greatest importance she realised from the fear in which his servants held him.

He had returned from Europe in time to quell a rebellion against his father, a rebellion which had brought about the death of his distinguished parent, and a multiplication of deaths amongst other parents not so distinguished, for Soo punished swiftly and terribly, and the execution ground outside the city walls ran red with blood as the executioner wielded his long, heavy sword.

On the third night of her arrival she was awakened by the Chinese maid, who signalled to her to rise. The girl would have dressed, but the servant snatched the clothes away.

"Puh p'a!" she said. ("You have nothing to fear".)

It was a conventional assurance, and the girl attached greater significance to the phrase than it deserved.

She was allowed to put on her dressing-gown, and thrust her feet into her slippers, and she followed the beckoning finger through the door.

There was nothing to be gained by resistance as she saw, for in the corridor outside were six men of the Yamen Guard.

With terror in her heart, but with her head erect, she followed the serving-maid through what seemed innumerable corridors until she came to a door before which hung a heavy curtain of orange velvet.

She had no idea as to what was the time. Her own watch had stopped, but from the glimpse of sky she caught as she passed a window, she thought it must be nearly three o'clock in the morning.

The servant pulled aside the portière and knocked timidly on the door, and a voice bade her enter.

Yvonne followed the girl. She was in a larger room than that to which she was accustomed. It was hung around with Chinese embroideries, the floor was of polished wood, and divans, cushions, and little stools formed the only furniture in the place, save for a few carved Buddhas and a huge hanging lamp suspended from the ceiling. It was unlit, the only light in the room being a small lamp placed on the floor within reach of Soo.

He was there alone, but what caught her eye and held her was something which stood in the very centre of the apartment.

It was a huge glass bottle, ten feet in height, and modelled in the shape of a medicine bottle. That, in fact, was the design which Soo had given to his artificers to cast.

The servant left her. The door closed with a click behind the girl, and she was left alone confronting this man with his cruel, smiling lips and his sly eyes.

He was smoking a Chinese pipe and was a model of comfort and self-satisfaction.

"I have sent for you," he said, "because you represent the last fragment of opposition offered to me in Europe, and I desire that you shall be disposed of with the ceremony which the occasion demands."

Planted against the bottle's neck was a light bamboo ladder; inside, dangling from the top, and secured from the outside by a ring fastened to the wall, was another ladder, a ladder of silk.

He saw her wondering eyes surveying this, and smiled.

"When I was in Europe," he said cheerfully, "there was a phrase employed which interested me more than ordinarily. It was the phrase of 'bottled up.' Now, I have never seen any human being so circumstanced."

He spoke slowly, choosing his words with great deliberation. "And I am particularly anxious that this reproach should be removed. You will mount those steps," he pointed to the ladder, "and lower yourself gently to the bottom of the bottle. You will notice that there is a down cushion upon which you may sit, and you will probably find it most comfortable."

"Suppose I refuse?" she said.

He smiled again.

"I think you will not refuse,"—he was very urbane, almost gentle of speech—"but if you do refuse, I will promise you that you shall be glad to have that bottle as a place of refuge."

He uttered two words sharply. The doors at the farther end of the apartment opened and four men came in naked to the waist—great muscular coolies with scarcely any humanity in their brutalised faces.

"Suppose," suggested Soo, "suppose, instead of putting you into the bottle and disposing of you as I shall in an especially novel fashion, I find a quicker death for you by handing you to these cattle?"

Her hands went to her face.

"No, no, no!" she shuddered.

At a nod from Soo the men departed.

"*Montez!*" said Soo mockingly, and she went up the creaking ladder without hesitation.

It said much for the immense size and solidity of the bottle that it did not budge under the strain of her weight. She sat for a moment on the edge of the neck with her feet dangling in the cavity where, in a bottle of ordinary dimensions, the cork would be fixed.

"Go on," said Soo, and glanced at the door.

She lowered herself with hands that shook down the swaying rope ladder, and came to rest on a cushion below.

She was in the room, but not of it. She saw Soo speaking but did not hear his voice till quite a second later, when it had travelled over the neck of the bottle and down to her. He came across and gave a pull upon the silk ladder and withdrew it flinging it down on the ground, and kicked the bamboo steps away. He spoke again, and his servants removed the only means by which she could escape.

She had to attune her ear to her strange position, and after a while, when she had learnt to ignore the movements of his lips and wait for the words to float down to her, she knew as well as though no solid wall of glass was between them.

He was sitting cross-legged on a cushion, still smoking his pipe. By and by he knocked the pipe out on to a little porcelain tray and devoted the whole of his attention to her.

"You may wonder," he said, "why I have awakened you at this inconvenient hour to begin a process which is to end your earthly career."

She made no reply.

"I do not doubt," he said, "that you expected sooner or later that your lover would learn of your unhappy plight and come hastening across China like a modern knight-errant to your rescue."

He spread out his hands in deprecation.

"Alas," he mocked, "your lover is not in a position to assist you, and far less is he in a position to assist himself."

"What do you mean?" she was startled into asking, and her voice sounded strange in that confined place.

"Alas!" repeated Soo. "He sits in the house of the dead, waiting for death."

She stared at him in horror.

He picked up another pipe and lit it from the tiny flame in the smoke-box by his side.

"He discovered the secret of the Emperor's tomb, you will be pleased to learn, and even penetrated its interior. I watched his interesting operations for close on an hour and a half without learning much, for the Emperor's tomb was known to me, and I might have forestalled him."

He thought awhile.

"It was better that he should do the work," he said, "and that I should have no more to do than to take the reward of his industry. I watched him enter, he and his Italian friend, and closed the door behind them. It was very simple, and was a matter of inductive reasoning, for the pulling on one silver lamp would open the door as the pulling on the second silver lamp would close it, since the robbers must find some way of veiling from the outside world the fact that they had been guilty of sacrilege. So it proved. Waiting there in the darkness whilst your friends were exploring the chamber below, I tested the second lamp and found that the door moved slowly. A dozen steps lay between them and liberty and life when I pulled with greater strength, and the door closed upon those inquisitive foreigners—that is all."

Something in his tone told her that he was speaking the truth. What hope was there now? In her heart of hearts she had depended upon Talham discovering her capture. If he were dead, nothing mattered. If all this man said was true, death could not come too quickly on her.

She sat crouched at the bottom of the bottle, her hands clasping her knees, her face fixed on his.

The end must come slowly if he spoke the truth. Soo was looking above the bottle thoughtfully: his gaze was fixed. She followed the direction of his eyes. From a round hole recently cut in the ceiling suspended a thick silken rope which hung directly over the mouth and came down to within a foot of the neck.

She had seen it before, and thought that it had been placed there to afford her assistance in making her entry into the bottle, whilst the ladder was removed, and still remained.

Soo's voice came to her soothingly.

"I see you have noticed it. That cord will give you some moments of interesting thought. Above this room is a smaller one, and in that small chamber is a large cage," he said, "and in that cage is a python. I presume you know what a python is. It is a snake of unusual size, and, in this particular case, unusually hungry. As to the habits of the python I am not well acquainted, but I hope to discover much interesting data from a closer observance than hitherto I have been able to secure."

He smiled.

She saw the smile almost before she had heard the last words.

"At your leisure"—he inclined his head—"you will clap your hands three times, and my servants, who will be on duty day and night, will release the reptile."

What did he mean?

She was soon to learn.

"I do not know what are the effects such confinement as yours will have upon you," he said, "but I rather think that after the end of twenty-four hours you may easily welcome the happy release, even though it be in so unpleasant a form."

He sat watching her with the drowsy eyes of a man under the influence of some narcotic. The sight of her fascinated him. All that was Oriental in him, all that loved suffering for suffering's sake, was alive to the possibilities which the situation offered. He had planned this end for her with such elaboration; and now found something wanting—something dramatic, something sudden.

Twenty-four hours was a long time, he might be sleeping when she gave the signal. She might die of fright or of exhaustion—these Western women were particularly fragile. Through the glass walls of her prison she watched the man, saw the curious look in his face, and knew instinctively that the respite he had given her he had already taken away. Something froze within her, her heart almost stopped beating as he raised his hand.

"I do not think I can afford to wait," he said apologetically.

He did not clap, for there came a slight knock at the door through which she had entered. He turned his frowning face to the portal.

"Come in!" he said quickly in Chinese.

It might be a message from the Mandarin of Hoo Sin. It might even be an Imperial rescript. The summons was not obeyed, and then he remembered that he had dropped the bar across the entrance. He rose slowly and walked across the room and slipped the lacquered bolt aside.

The sliding doors slipped apart, and Captain Talham stepped into the room, a revolver in each hand.

This the girl saw, and fainted.

CHAPTER 20

SOO "SAVES-FACE"

LEFT alone in the darkness of the tomb the two men stood motionless. Til-lizinni was the first to realise the awfulness of their position. None knew the secret of the door save themselves.

The men at the foot of the hill, if they were not already destroyed by Soo's soldiers, would wait til the morning, and then with true Chinese philosophy would report the occurrence to the Mandarin of Hoo Sin.

By that time the two pioneers would be dead.

There was very little air in the chasm, and apparently no inlet. The door itself was almost hermetically sealed; they would exhaust the supply which they had unconsciously brought in with them in less than an hour. Talham was the first to recover himself. He ran up the remainder of the steps until he came to the blank wall of the silver door and carefully examined its face with his lamp. The two edges of the door fitted in a flange, and there was no place where a lever, even if they had possessed one, could have found a purchase. As it happened, they had left all their tools at the bronze door.

"Keep to the spirit steps," said Talham, "and go down below again. We may find something there. I think you will have plenty of opportunity, at any rate," he added grimly, "to discover the lighting secret of this place."

Back they went again to the chamber of the dead. The little quicksilver rivers were running merrily, as they had for two thousand years, and they might run for all eternity until through countless thousands of years the quicksilver became volatised.

There were stacks of ancient arms placed near the stone door, but none of these would be of any use to the men.

They made a diligent search for some other means of exit, but in vain. There was no time to waste in purely scientific exploration.

They had obviated the necessity for one of them standing on the lower step, by lifting thereon one of the heavy irons which stood at the four corners of the pedestal, and this weight was apparently sufficient to keep the light going.

"I'm afraid we're caught," said Talham at last, and Tillizinni nodded.

It was a curious end to all his extraordinary adventures, yet if an end could be attractive, surely this was one, to go down in this treasure-house of the past—to go out in the shadow of the great Emperor's tomb.

A romancer to the finger-tips, Tillizinni found some consolation in the prospect, but Talham was devoid of sentiment.

"It isn't the death I mind," he said quietly; "but we ought not to have come, we should have made straight for Yvonne. We know she is in that fiend's power; how could I have been so mad as to have neglected her for one moment—all the treasures in the world were not worth it."

On one of the steps he had placed the jade box. He lifted it up and looked at it resentfully, and raising it above his head he sent it crashing down amongst the artificial landscape which covered one half of the floor. The box burst and a roll of parchment fell out.

"Leave it alone," said Talham roughly, "there is only one thing in the world that counts."

He did not say what that one thing was, but Tillizinni guessed. Another examination of the chamber offered no better result. At the foot of the bier Tillizinni found a square box, which he prised open without any difficulty. It was filled to the brim with pearls of varying sizes from that of the average pea to pearls as large as pigeons' eggs.

If only they could make their escape from here the box would represent an enormous fortune.

If Talham despised the secret of the philosopher, here might be some compensation for all his trouble if they made their escape. The chances were very slight, but——

Tillizinni took a handful of the gems, and put them in the loose pocket of his coat. He took another and another, until the pocket bulged.

He made his way back with difficulty to where Talham stood by the lower step. The air was getting foul, and he found a difficulty in breathing; the end would come very soon—the scientist in him told him that.

"Have you found anything?"

Talham did not answer.

He was looking stupidly at one of the two ornaments which flanked the lower steps leading into the death chamber.

"What is it?" asked Tillizinni.

Talham nodded sleepily.

Tillizinni examined the object of his interest a little closer.

It was one of the two huge birds of bronze. It seemed alive as it stood there, balanced on one leg.

"I didn't notice those before," said Talham. Neither had the other, a fact easily explained as they stood in the shadow cast by the two great War Gods which towered left and right of the tomb's entrance.

"I think this is where we go out," muttered Talham. His heart was beating at a terrific rate; his head was swimming. He was affected sooner than the smaller man, and staggered, and would have fallen but for Tillizinni's arm.

"You had better sit down," said Tillizinni quietly.

He would take his own advice later; seated with his back to the wall he would wait for death.

But Talham shook his head; he took a step and swayed, reached out his hand to steady himself, and caught the bronze bird by the neck.

He threw his head back suddenly.

"A pelican," he said thickly. "A pelican! my God! I didn't see a pelican——"

There was no other word. He threw all his weight upon the neck of the bronze bird, and it bent down towards him as if working upon an invisible pivot.

There was a rumble at the head of the stairs; a draught of sweet, fresh air rushed down to the men, and Talham fell on his hands and knees and breathed it in greedily.

"So that was it," he gasped. "Now, Soo, look out for me!" and he went reeling up the stairs like a drunken man, Tillizinni following.

They went out into the starlit night to find their patient men still sitting in the gulley waiting for orders.

Whilst the men were mounting, Talham went back to the tomb alone. He was absent for five minutes.

"Oughtn't we do something to hide the door?" asked Tillizinni. "There will be an awful row when it is found open."

Talham turned on his saddle.

"It will be hidden in a minute," he said.

At that moment there was a dull, muffled roar which set the horses prancing.

"I dynamited the first chamber," said Talham "That's the end of the Emperor's tomb."

* * * *

Soo stared blankly at the intruder, but he did not lose his presence of mind.

"Captain Talham, I believe," he said. "How very interesting!"

He smiled at the stern-faced man before him.

"I had intended coming to-morrow to find your unhappy bodies"—he saw Tillizinni at the entrance and nodded in a friendly way—"and incidentally to help myself to such of the treasures of the great Emperor's. May he dwell in the seventeenth heaven for a million years"—he bowed his head in mock reverence; "but that one pleasure, at least, is deferred."

"All your pleasures are deferred," said Talham sternly. "You will never again discover the tomb of the dead Emperor—neither you nor any other man. The outer chamber has ceased to be."

Soo lifted his eyebrows.

"Indeed!" he said incredulously.

"I have dynamited the entrance," said Talham in his thorough way. "That ends the business of the Emperor's tomb, and——"

Then it was that he saw the bottle. The room was in half darkness as he had entered; only one faint light showed, and this was beside the place where Soo had sat.

The reflection of the light upon the polished face of the glass prevented him from seeing its interior. He took a step forward.

"My God!" he said. "Yvonne!"

He turned and pointed the revolver at the other's head. His face was white and drawn.

"Damn you!" he said.

"She is not dead—she is alive," said Soo quickly.

"Alive!" Talham dropped his revolver.

"For the moment, yes," said Soo, and clasped his hands.

Talham heard the shriek of the girl, saw the wild agony in her face, and realised that this was a signal for some act of treachery. But it was Tillizinni who saw the dangling rope, and heard the rustle of a heavy body moving on the floor above. It was Tillizinni who saw the wedge-shaped head with the cruel, cold eyes peep down through the hole and stretch out its sinuous body towards the rope.

He knew instantly the significance of that dangling cord.

"Quick!" he cried, and threw the whole of his weight against the bottle. It slid over the polished floor a dozen paces.

"Stop him!" said Tillizinni.

Soo was making for the door. He turned when the revolvers were levelled, and lifted his hands.

"There will be no trouble," he said.

Even in that moment of his deadly peril he did not lose his nerve. He seemed to take a delight in recalling the suavities of his Western veneer.

"I am quite prepared to stand my trial before the Imperial Court for anything I have done," he said. "In the meantime, will you allow me to summon my men to assist your friend from her distressing position?"

"We will do without the servants," said Tillizinni. "Get some of those cushions, quick!"

They laid three thicknesses of down cushions before the bottle, the way it would fall.

Then Tillizinni deftly wedged the front and the two men threw their weight on it. It fell over unbroken, and the girl dragged her way out.

"Take her outside," said Tillizinni, and Talham lifted the half-fainting figure and bore her from the room along the deserted corridors to the little courtyard behind, where his men were waiting.

The Yamen was wrapped in slumber; Soo had given orders that he was not to be disturbed that night, and beyond a watchman who had been at the gate, but who was now no longer in a position to hinder the party, there was none to say them nay.

Tillizinni confronted Soo T'si, and if ever there were two men in the world competent to deal with one another in that extreme crisis, they were those two, who now stood face to face.

Ever and anon, Tillizinni's eyes would go up to the little round hole in the roof. He had recognised the head the moment he had seen it, and knew that the python was searching for food in the room above, until, in his desperation, he took the more desperate step of descending the rope.

"Soo T'si," said Tillizinni gently, "you will find it much easier to get into the bottle than, I gather, did Miss Yale."

"It is possible," said the Chinaman coolly; "but it is not an experiment that I care to make."

"It is an experiment," said Tillizinni in the same tone, "which I shall ask you to make, for if you do not do as I tell you, I shall most certainly shoot you."

Soo shrugged his shoulders.

"You should have been a Chinaman," he said.

"I am of the race," said Tillizinni carefully, "which produced the Borgias, and some of the most refined torturers of the Holy Inquisition. Enter your bottle, my friend!" he said. "I wish to see you bottled up in reality. You will find the place cramped, but you will probably be able to bear the indignity of it much easier than the delicate and refined English lady whom we have just released."

"I will do anything," said Soo, "save sacrifice my dignity."

His eyes followed the other to a little aperture in the roof. The head of the python was hanging down now; his hateful eyes surveyed them.

"I see your idea," said Soo pleasantly. "I think I know a better way. A Chinaman must 'save face,' you know!"

His hands were concealed under his silken jacket. Tillizinni could not see the man searching for the razor-like knife which he carried at his waistband, nor the firm fingers of the suicide feeling for the little place under the heart which, skilfully pierced, brings an easy death. Only he saw the face go suddenly grey.

"Au 'voir," said Soo in French. "I like this way better."

He fell in a heap on the ground, and looked up with a smile.

"Pardon—me!" he said, smiling faintly—and died.

So Tillizinni left him, with the head of the python looking hungrily down on the quiet figure below. So Tillizinni thinks of this man now, and often sees him at night—a smiling, fearless figure of a villain.

And when all the lights are lit upon the Embankment, and Tillizinni leans out of his window watching the dark river and the flaming lamps of London, he looks westward and tries to picture Captain Talham a happy, domesticated man in his Surbiton home, with his motorcars and his race horses and all the good things of life which the Emperor's pearls had brought to him.

Somehow Tillizinni fails to reconcile those two men. The Talham who held the fort of Hoo Sin against the armed soldiery of Tai Pan come to avenge their lord; the Talham who made the wild flight across China to the link of civilisation which the Siberian railway afforded, with the Talham who now discusses poultry and pigs with such earnestness and volubility.

"For my part," wrote Tillizinni in his diary, "I would as lief be buried alive in the tomb under Mount Li, as be buried alive in a suburb of London."

It is, of course, a matter of opinion.

www.ingramcontent.com/pod-product-compliance
Lightning Source LLC
Chambersburg PA
CBHW011437170626
46808CB00009B/3079